There was silence for ____
there was a problem w ____

*Rose asked, "And so what happens if you get pregnant, and you're
too young to actually have a baby?"*

*Defying all laws of inertia, the acceleration of Kennedy's heart
rate crashed to a halt like a car plowing into a brick wall. "What
do you mean?"*

"Like, what if you're too young but you still get pregnant?"

*"How young?" Kennedy spoke both words clearly and slowly, as
if rushing might drive the timid voice away for good.*

"Like thirteen."

Praise for *Unplanned*
by Alana Terry

"Deals with **one of the most difficult situations a pregnancy center
could ever face**. The message is **powerful** and the story-
telling **compelling**." ~ William Donovan, *Executive Director
Anchorage Community Pregnancy Center*

"Alana Terry does an amazing job tackling a very **sensitive subject
from the mother's perspective**." ~ Pamela McDonald, *Director
Okanogan CareNet Pregnancy Center*

"**Thought-provoking** and intense ... Shows **different sides of the
abortion argument**." ~ Sharee Stover, *Wordy Nerdy*

"Alana has a way of sharing the gospel **without being preachy**." ~
Phyllis Sather, *Purposeful Planning*

She wouldn't be victimized again. She had to get away. She wouldn't let him catch up to her. A footstep on the concrete. Not a fabrication. Not this time. It was real. Real as the scientific method. Real as her parents' love for her. Real as death. In the pitch darkness, she rushed ahead, running her fingers along the grimy wall so she would know which way to go as she sprinted down the walkway. What did contracting a few germs compare to getting murdered?

How close was he now? And why couldn't she have remembered her pepper spray? She strained her ears but only heard the slap of her boots on the walkway, the sound of her own panting, the pounding of her heart valves in her pericardial sac. She didn't want to stop, couldn't slow down, but she had to save her strength. She needed energy to fight back when he caught up. She couldn't hear him, but that didn't mean he wasn't coming.

Any second now.

Praise for *Paralyzed*
by Alana Terry

"Alana Terry has **done the almost unthinkable**; she has written a story with **raw emotions of real people**, not the usual glossy Christian image." ~ Jasmine Augustine, Tell Tale Book Reviews

"Alana has a way of **using fiction to open difficult issues** and make you think." ~ Phyllis Sather, Author of *Purposeful Planning*

"Once again, Ms. Terry brings a **sensitive but important issue to the forefront** without giving an answer. She **leaves it up to the reader** to think about and decide." ~ Darla Meyer, Book Reviewer

Without warning, the officer punched Reuben in the gut. Reuben doubled over as the cop brought his knee up to his face. Reuben staggered.

"You dirty n—." Without warning, the cop whipped out his pistol and smashed its butt against Reuben's head. He crumpled to the ground, where the officer's boots were ready to meet him with several well-placed kicks.

Throwing all rational thoughts aside, Kennedy jumped on his back. Anything to get him to stop beating Reuben. The officer swore and swatted at her. Kennedy heard herself screaming but had no idea what she was saying. She couldn't see anything else, nor could she understand how it was that when her normal vision returned, she was lying on her back, but the officer and Reuben were nowhere to be seen.

Praise for *Policed*
by Alana Terry

"*Policed* could be taken **from the headlines of today's news**." ~ Meagan Myhren-Bennett, *Blooming with Books*

"**A provocative story** with authentic characters." ~ Sheila McIntyre, *Book Reviewer*

"It is important for Christian novelists to address today's issues like police misconduct and racism. Too often writers tiptoe around **serious issues faced by society**." ~ Wesley Harris, *Law Enforcement Veteran*

"Focuses on a prevalent issue in today's society. Alana **pushes the boundaries more than any other Christian writer**." ~ Angie Stormer, *Readaholic Zone*

Wayne Abernathy, the Massachusetts state senator, was towering over a teenage boy who sat crumpled over the Lindgrens' dining room table.

"I don't care what you have to do to fix him," Wayne blasted at Carl.

Kennedy froze. Nobody heard her enter. Carl sat with his back to her, but she could still read the exhaustion in his posture.

Wayne brought his finger inches from the boy's nose. "Do whatever you have to do, Pastor. Either straighten him up, or so help me, he's got to find some other place to live."

Kennedy bit her lip, trying to decide if it would be more awkward to leave, make her presence known, or stay absolutely still.

Wayne's forehead beaded with sweat, and his voice quivered with conviction. "It's impossible for any son of mine to turn out gay."

Praise for *Straightened*
by Alana Terry

"Alana doesn't take a side, but she makes you really think. She **presents both sides of the argument in a very well written way**." ~ Diane Higgins, *The Book Club Network*

"No matter what conviction you have on the subject, I'm fairly certain **you will find that this novel has a character who accurately represents that viewpoint**." ~ Justin, Avid Reader

"Alana Terry doesn't beat up her readers, but, rather she gets them to either examine their own beliefs or encourages them to **find out for themselves what they believe and what the Bible says**." ~ Jasmine Augustine, *Tell Tale Book Reviews*

She shook her head. "I don't know. I can't say. I just know that something is wrong here. It's not safe." She clenched his arm with white knuckles. "Please, I can't ... We have to ..." She bit her lip.

He frowned and let out a heavy sigh. "You're absolutely certain?"

She nodded faintly. "I think so."

"It's probably just nerves. It's been a hard week for all of us." There was a hopefulness in his voice but resignation in his eyes.

She sucked in her breath. "This is different. Please." She drew her son closer to her and lowered her voice. "For the children."

"All right." He unbuckled his seatbelt and signaled one of the flight attendants. "I'm so sorry to cause a problem," he told her when she arrived in the aisle, "but you need to get my family off this plane. Immediately."

Praise for *Turbulence*
by Alana Terry

"This book is **hard to put down** and is a **suspenseful roller coaster of twists and turns**." ~ Karen Brooks, *The Book Club Network*

"I've enjoyed all of the Kennedy Stern novels so far, but **this one got to me in a more personal way** than the others have." ~ *Fiction Aficionado*

"I love that the author is **not afraid to deal with tough issues all believers deal with**." ~ Kit Hackett, *YWAM Missionary*

Note: The views of the characters in this novel do not necessarily reflect the views of the author, nor is their behavior necessarily condoned.

The characters in this book are fictional. Any resemblance to real persons is coincidental. No part of this book may be reproduced in any form (electronic, audio, print, film, etc.) without the author's written consent.

Secluded

a novel by Alana Terry

"Praise the Lord, my soul; all my inmost being, praise his holy name. Praise the Lord, my soul, and forget not all his benefits— who forgives all your sins and heals all your diseases."

Psalm 103:1-3

CHAPTER 1

11:48 pm, the day before the Winter Solstice

"I can't believe Nick and I are actually getting married!" Willow squealed.

Kennedy listened to her roommate through a thick fog of jet lag-induced exhaustion. Driving five hours in the dark wasn't how she'd planned to spend her first night of Christmas vacation in Alaska. She took a sip of what had once been hot cocoa and was now a grainier version of chocolate milk.

"I'm really excited for you." Kennedy hoped her voice held the right amount of enthusiasm. If she thought Willow and Nick's engagement came suddenly, it was nothing compared to how fast they'd set the date.

The day after tomorrow, just a few days before Christmas, Willow and Nick would exchange their vows in the little

1

country church near Willow's childhood home in Copper Lake, a small homestead community about forty-five minutes beyond Glennallen and the edge of the Glenn Highway.

Willow drummed her mittens on the steering wheel to keep time with her classic rock music. "I'm so glad you're here. I couldn't ask for a better maid of honor."

Kennedy had never been in a wedding before and could only guess what she was expected to do. Her roommate assured her the ceremony would be a casual event and she had nothing to worry about, but Willow obviously didn't understand the way Kennedy's brain worked.

There was always something to worry about.

Like the way her friend Ian had asked her out on several breakfast dates before his business trip to Asia and hadn't called or emailed or texted her since.

Or like the way she'd been fired from her TA job last semester because she refused to take back what she'd written for a column in the school paper. The details regarding how she'd been treated after publishing her piece in the Harvard Forum had made little waves in pro First Amendment blogs and news outlets, but the publicity was finally starting to die down, thank God.

"Oh!" Willow exclaimed. "I almost forgot. You were going to answer some of those questions I had about

Revelations, remember?"

Kennedy remembered, but she was exhausted after three different flights and two drawn-out layovers, not to mention all the strange events that had happened since she landed in Alaska. There was no way she could muster up the energy it'd take to field all of Willow's questions about the end times. She should be asleep in a nice Anchorage hotel right now like she'd originally planned, not making the five-hour drive to Copper Lake this late at night.

Willow turned her music down. "All right. First question is about the rapture. I basically know what it means, at least I think I do. It's when Jesus comes back and takes all the believers up to heaven, right?"

Kennedy was pining away for a soft pillow and layer upon layer of blankets. Even with the heat running in Willow's car, she hadn't been able to shake her chill since arriving in Alaska. The outside temperature had dropped below negative twenty once they approached the mountain pass on the Glenn Highway. Kennedy had decided that all the handmade quilts Willow's family owned still wouldn't be enough to warm her entirely.

Or help her forget her fears from that night.

"… why some people argue that the rapture's got to happen first but others say it won't come until later, and

3

when I went to study it for myself, the word *rapture* wasn't even in the New Testament, so that's my first question."

Kennedy tried to figure out what she'd missed. The rapture? She didn't know how to respond. She'd read through Revelation once or maybe twice before, but she always stepped into it assuming it would be too hard to grasp, a prediction that turned into a self-fulfilling prophecy. She liked the last couple chapters that talked about having no more death or crying or pain in heaven, and she figured that the letters to the churches at the beginning of the book had some good advice for believers today, but all the stuff in the middle was so wrapped up in convoluted symbolism that she never bothered trying to make sense out of it.

If experts who'd been studying theology for hundreds of years couldn't agree, how could Kennedy presume to understand? Jesus would come back, and all believers would end up in heaven. The rest of the details were best left for pastors and seminary professors to discuss and debate.

Still, she owed Willow some sort of response, but unfortunately her brain had already shut down for the night. Her roommate had been growing so fast in her faith, Kennedy was scrambling to catch up.

"And then there's the tribulation," Willow went on. Maybe if she talked long enough, she would eventually land on a question Kennedy felt qualified to answer. "I read one commentator who said the tribulation's just this sort of symbolic idea that Christians are going to suffer before Jesus returns, but then Pastor Carl was talking in his sermon about how it's this literal seven-year period, and either way you look at it is pretty depressing."

Kennedy muttered some sort of response about how that was a good point and wondered what else she could contribute to the conversation.

Willow moved on to the millennium, but Kennedy was only half listening. After everything she'd experienced in Anchorage that night, it was understandable for her to feel more than a little edgy. The sun had already set by the time her plane touched down that afternoon, and now it was even darker. No street lamps, no light pollution because they were on that stretch of the Glenn Highway where you could travel fifty or sixty miles between towns.

She shouldn't be worried about the dark. That was just her anxiety kicking in. She'd picked the second shortest day of the year to land in Alaska, and the entire state felt on the verge of panic. Of course, the increasingly vocal number of wackos claiming that the winter solstice would mark the beginning of some sort of Armageddon-like end-of-days scenario did nothing to settle her nerves, not to mention the recent events that seemed to verify their predictions.

She wouldn't think about that. If she knew anything about what the Bible said, it was that nobody could guess the time or the day of Christ's return. Everyone claiming something contrary was making stuff up, even the ones who seemed to forecast with uncanny accuracy the meteorological events that had been popping up worldwide.

An F-4 tornado in the Midwest in December. An unseasonably late typhoon hitting the Philippines that same week, and that was on top of everything going on in Alaska.

Her dad had warned her, hadn't he? Said that even if the geological predictions weren't accurate, the civil unrest that could ensue from such wild claims would make the state volatile. Dangerous.

He hadn't told her not to go. She was too old to be ordered around like that, and he knew how much it meant to her to be the maid of honor at her roommate's wedding. But he'd asked her several times to reconsider.

When she came here with Willow in the past, Alaska felt so quiet, so safe. Should she have listened to her dad? Well, it was too late now. All the planes were grounded, so it's not like she could change her mind even if she wanted to.

At least Copper Lake was far enough removed from the

chaos. Hopefully.

No, she shouldn't think like that. She had to be more positive.

"So I'm leaning towards what Sproul says when it comes to the millennium, but I'm still planning to read up a little more on it. What do you think?"

Kennedy frantically tried to replay the last few lines of conversation.

"You weren't listening were you?" Willow accused.

"I was listening," Kennedy protested. "I heard what you were saying, I just didn't …" She tried to find the right words.

"Didn't pay attention?" Willow let out a good-natured chuckle.

Kennedy stared at her lap. "Sorry."

"It's ok. It's been a wicked long day for you, hasn't it?"

"That's one way of putting it." Kennedy had been looking forward to spending Christmas break in Alaska, not just because she was excited to share in all the wedding plans but because Copper Lake was so peaceful. Maybe spending a week or two with the Winters each year was the cure for her anxiety that she'd been hunting for. But now, after everything that had happened in one short evening …

"Well, we can discuss Revelations later, all right?"

Willow turned off her classic rock music. "Let's talk about something else. Like what did you think of the movie? At least the parts we got to see."

Kennedy didn't want to admit she'd been too tired to pay attention when they were at the theater earlier. The end-times flick Willow had dragged her to was horribly canned. "It was all right."

Willow turned the music off. "Do you think it really could happen like that, with them rounding up the Christians and taking away all the Bibles?"

At least this was a question Kennedy felt somewhat qualified to answer after the ten years she spent with her parents in China. "It's like that already in some parts of the world. I told you the story about that Bible smuggler from North Korea, right?"

"Yeah. So I guess we just need to be prepared to die for our faith one day?"

The question surprised Kennedy. "I suppose so. At least theoretically."

"And what about people like that mother in the movie, the one who pretended to go along with them and got that chip in her hand and said she didn't believe in Jesus? It wasn't like she meant it. She just told them that so they wouldn't take her baby away from her. God wouldn't send

8

her to hell over something like that, right?"

Now they had officially crossed into territory in which Kennedy was too tired and too inexperienced to offer any kind of reasonable answer. "I really don't think it's a question of heaven or hell. It's just doing what God thinks you should do and knowing that despite everything he's watching you and he'll be with you."

Apparently, Willow wasn't satisfied with Kennedy's rambling response. "Ok, let me put it another way. Let's say that she stood up for her beliefs, that she didn't let them put in that chip and she didn't deny Christ, so then she gets thrown in jail and her daughter gets handed over to the atheist family. What then? Does God promise that at some point he'll make sure the little girl will grow up and learn the truth? Because otherwise, if you're asking a mother to either lie about her own faith or surrender her kid to hell ..."

Kennedy was glad Willow's voice trailed off. Glad there wasn't an actual question she was expected to answer. As a result of her parents' work with underground Christians, Kennedy had heard harrowing stories of the suffering believers endured, but she did her best to compartmentalize them as things that happened on the other side of the world to people who looked and spoke and lived entirely differently than she did.

"Anyway," Willow added, "I thought the policeman was wicked hot. And I've seen him in something else, but I can't remember what. Maybe that hospital drama on HBO? Was he on there?"

Kennedy was relieved at the conversational turn. While Willow rambled on about different TV shows, Kennedy could stare out the window at the blinding darkness without having to think.

"... she's the one in that super cute detective series. You know which one I mean?"

Kennedy snapped her head around. "Huh?"

Willow sighed. "How about you pick something to talk about? I'm out of ideas."

Kennedy's hands grew sweaty even though her core was chilled. What should she say? That after everything that had happened since she arrived in Alaska, it was taking every bit of her mental energy to keep from panicking? That she was starting to wonder if she should have listened to her dad even if it meant missing out on Willow's big day? That knowing all the flights in and out of Anchorage were grounded made her feel claustrophobic in spite of how large this state was, and driving in the pitch dark in the snow in sub-zero temperatures was one of the creepiest things she'd done all year.

No, she couldn't focus on her fear. Even if she was stuck here in Alaska, even if the dire predictions made by these end-of-the-worlders with their picket signs came true, it's not like she could turn around now, hop on a plane, and fly back East. There was nothing to do but make the best of her situation and focus on positive things.

Like Willow getting ready to marry the love of her life.

"How are things going back home?" she asked. "What do your parents think of Nick?"

"Oh, they love him to pieces." Willow ran her fingers through her hair, which she'd reverted back to its natural color for the wedding. Up until now Kennedy thought it was those outrageous dye jobs that made Willow stand out in a crowd, but now she realized her roommate would look stunning no matter what she did with her hair. "You should have heard Nick and my dad last night. They were talking about everything that's been happening, then got onto global warming and carbon footprints and climate change. I swear if I weren't going to marry him, my dad would do it for me."

"Do they have any problems with him being a Christian?"

Willow shook her feathery head of hair. "Not at all. My mom thinks those goofy shirts of his are adorable, and he and my parents are always having really deep discussions

11

about faith and politics — you know, all those things that Nick hates talking about," she added with a sarcastic grin.

Kennedy hoped her chuckle sounded convincing. "Well, I'm glad he's fitting in so well."

"Me too. I think my only real complaint is that my parents don't see the difference between me being a Christian and me falling in love with Nick. The way they look at it, they assume I converted because of him."

"But you got saved before you and Nick met."

Willow shrugged. "Yeah, I know, but in their minds it's all one big life event. But it's not that bad. They're really happy for me. They know I've been taking my faith seriously, and I think it's been good for them to meet Nick, who's so different from the typical Christian you see in sitcoms or read about in the news, you know?" She laughed. "I'm just glad that they're so comfortable with him. I swear they act like he's their long-lost son or something."

"What about Nick's family?" Kennedy asked. "Are many of them coming up for the wedding? Did anybody get stuck before they could fly in?"

"No, it's so cold up here we didn't want to make everyone fly out. We'll head to Washington right after Christmas, assuming the planes are up and running by then."

Kennedy calmed the quivering in her core. Tried to

forget everything that had happened to spook her once she'd arrived in Alaska. Did her best to convince herself that Copper Lake was far enough from Anchorage that she'd be perfectly fine. By the time she was ready to fly back East to spend Christmas with her pastor's family, everything would be back to normal again.

She hoped.

"What about you?" Willow asked.

"Me what?"

"I don't know. Tell me about your finals or about your premed stuff or about Mr. Redhead who's taken you out to breakfast like five times this semester. I've been doing nothing but listen to Nick and my dad talk politics for the past week. I need some kind of distraction."

Kennedy tried to think of something interesting to tell her roommate that she didn't already know. She had spent most of the past semester wondering about her relationship with Ian and stressing out about med school. Her provisional acceptance to Harvard's program had been revoked after she wrote a newspaper article that turned out to be far more controversial than she'd expected. It had taken both her dad and her reporter friend Ian several different phone calls to several different news outlets to convince the university to change their minds. Thanks to their concerted effort, she had a guaranteed spot in Harvard Med School once she graduated, but did she want to go anymore? Why should she come crawling back to the administration that slammed their doors in her face for doing nothing but stating her opinion?

The question had reverberated in the back of her head all semester. Unfortunately, it was a decision she couldn't postpone indefinitely. By summer at the latest, she'd have to decide. It wasn't like her to be without a solid, definitive course of action. As much as she trusted God's guidance, she needed a plan, a plan that preferably laid out the next five to ten years in a neat, tidy package.

As for Ian ...

"You can start that conversation any time, you know."

Kennedy snapped back to the present. "What were we talking about?"

"That's what you were supposed to decide, remember?"

"Oh, yeah. Umm ..." Kennedy stared at the snowflakes illuminated in Willow's headlights. "Let's see ... Is everything ready for the big day?"

Willow laughed. "I'm going to be so sick of planning weddings when this is all over. I can guarantee you that. Sandy called me a few nights ago to see how things were coming along. It was really sweet of her. I joked and told her if I'd known how stressful it was to plan even a simple wedding like ours, Nick and I would have eloped months ago. But she reminded me how special it is to be engaged, and something about that gave me more perspective, I guess. I mean, every single day that we have to keep ourselves pure is a new adventure in self-control, but here we are, and in two days we'll be husband and wife, so it's not like waiting was the end of the world.

"Oh, speaking of the end of the world, that was another question I wanted to ask you. The mark of the beast. Is the number 666 some really crazy dangerous thing like some people say? I mean, I saw it mentioned there in Revelations and they talked about it a lot in that movie, but I wasn't sure if it was the number itself that was so evil or if it's more symbolic or whatnot."

Kennedy wished she could transport herself through time and space and end up at the Winters' homestead in Copper Lake, hopefully beneath ten or twelve quilts. "I don't know."

Willow glanced over at her, clearly expecting more.

"I don't know," she repeated. "I seriously have no idea."

Willow frowned and finally shrugged. "Fair enough." She sighed. "I kind of want to call Nick and see how he's doing, but we won't have cell coverage for quite a while." She pointed at the time. "Hey, look. We made it to midnight." She cracked a huge grin. "Happy solstice."

15

Kennedy wasn't sure if the greeting was an Alaskan tradition or something her roommate came up with. "You too," she replied tentatively.

Willow let out a carefree laugh. "Looks like the end-of-the-worlders were wrong again. I'm still here. Are you?"

"Yeah." Kennedy tried to sound amused, but she was still thinking about how worried her dad had been about her traveling to Alaska in the first place.

Willow started to hum under her breath, and Kennedy chuckled when she recognized the tune.

"Don't tease me," Willow protested. "Can't I be excited without you making fun of me?"

Kennedy giggled. It felt nice to stop focusing on Alaskan crises and apocalyptic predictions and bizarre meteorological phenomena. Willow was getting married in two days, and Kennedy was going to toss aside her worries long enough to give her roommate the celebration she deserved.

Willow increased her volume, and Kennedy started singing with her.

Because we're going to the chapel ...

Before long, they were both belting as loudly as they could, making up in enthusiasm what they lacked in musical ability.

And we're gonna get married.

Their singing was terrible, but the stress of the day coupled with her exhaustion made it seem that much funnier. Kennedy couldn't hold in her laugh.

That's when she heard Willow scream.

Saw the massive animal directly in front of them.

Felt the seatbelt yank against her chest as the car plowed into a moose.

CHAPTER 2

3:48 pm, seven hours earlier

For Alaska's biggest city, Anchorage looked tiny from this high up. Kennedy leaned toward the window of the plane. A full day of traveling, and she was ready to be on land.

Her junior year of college was whizzing by. Wasn't it only a few months ago she'd flown into Boston for the first time, a scared little eighteen-year-old girl who could have never been prepared for all the excitement, adventure, heartache and growth she was about to experience at Harvard?

Her course load was easier now than it had ever been, especially after losing her job as a teaching assistant. She devoted her extra free time to volunteering for the afterschool club for students at Medford Academy, trying to get more involved at St. Margaret's Church, and daydreaming with Willow about her wedding.

She couldn't believe how fast the big day was approaching. She thought about the phone call she'd had with her dad this morning while she waited for her first flight to take off from Logan Airport.

"You still think it's going to be safe over there, Kensie girl?" he asked.

Kennedy was certain that even from China he could see her roll her eyes. "It's going to be fine. They've been talking about this volcano for weeks now. It's not that big of a deal. And it's nowhere near Copper Lake."

"No," he replied, "but it's near Anchorage. When that mountain blows, the ash will cover the city in an hour, two at most."

"It's just a little dust, Dad." What did he think? That a volcano a hundred miles away would rain lava down on them?

"It's dust that's going to clog up car engines, ground planes, and potentially cause a major panic. Anchorage isn't Yanji or Boston, but it's still a big city, Kensie girl. And worst case scenario, if something does happen there, even if you're with the Winters already, that means no food trucks, no supplies being brought into the rural areas."

"I can't miss Willow's wedding."

He sighed. "Well, I won't tell you what to do, but if you go, you've got to be extra careful. Like I said, if that volcano blows, you need to get out of Anchorage right away. Promise me that much, at least."

"Yeah, I promise."

"Good. So your plane lands around four, and then you're driving with Willow to her home?"

Now it was Kennedy's turn to let out a massive sigh. Did her dad expect her to recite every single calorie she planned on eating in Alaska too? "We're spending the night in Anchorage. It's already going to be dark by the time I land, and Willow has some shopping to do in town anyway."

"I don't like that plan," her dad announced, as if that simple statement should be enough to change her mind.

"I already told you, if the volcano erupts, we'll get on the road before the ash falls."

"What if you're asleep?" he demanded.

Then I'm sure you'll find a way to call or text or wake me up, she thought to herself but instead just answered, "We'll be fine."

"It's not only the volcano I'm worried about, you know. Those winter solstice guys, they're all convinced that the end of the world's going to start tomorrow."

"They're just a bunch of weirdos," Kennedy protested. Her dad might be paranoid, but he certainly wasn't so removed from reality that he gave credence to their ideas, did he?

"I know that, and you know that, but what about all the people they've got so freaked out? What's going to happen when that volcano erupts and these internet junkies use it to fuel all the fear and chaos they've been creating? I just don't want to see you in harm's way."

"Yeah, ok." What else was there she could say?

"Yeah ok what?" he asked.

"I'll be careful."

"That's all I can ask," he replied with an air of defeat.

CHAPTER 3

Past midnight, Winter Solstice

"You all right in there? Hey, you all right?"

Cold. Kennedy had never been so cold in her life.

"You ok?" There was a pounding on the car window, a flashlight beam blinding her eyes.

She reached her hand to the side and croaked weakly, "Willow?"

"I'm here."

A small breath of warmth when her fingertips brushed her roommate's shoulder.

"We're ok?" Kennedy asked.

"Yeah, we're ok. We hit a moose."

"I know. I saw it."

"Me, too. Just too late."

More tapping on the window. "Can you hear me? Do you need help?"

"Someone's here," Kennedy announced. Feeling was returning to her limbs. Limbs that ached as if frost had seeped into each individual nerve bundle. How long had she and Willow been lying here? She tried her door and did her best to rouse up her energy. There was a fierce pain in her neck and shoulder, but she didn't think anything was broken. Her leg was pinned beneath the crumpled dashboard, but it didn't hurt. Just felt cold.

Terribly cold.

"Unlock the door!" The shout was muffled. He had to repeat himself several times before Kennedy fully understood.

She undid the locks, and the man opened the driver's side. The cold burst in through the open door and settled in her bone marrow.

"You hurt?" He shined his flashlight into the car, studying both girls' faces, then checked the backseat. "Just the two of you? Are you all right?"

"My leg's stuck," Kennedy told him.

"What about you?" He turned to Willow.

"Yeah. I'm ok. Just a little ..." She shook her head slightly. "Dude."

"You black out?" he asked. "How long you been here?"

Willow looked at Kennedy, who had no answer to give.

"It's ok," the man said. "Listen, there's no reception here, but I live about six miles out. I can give you a ride to my place and we can get you warmed up. Don't want to take the time to call for help and wait for the ambulance to come if we don't got to. It's minus twenty-eight last I checked. Nothing broken that you can tell?"

Willow had already adjusted herself loose while he was talking. Kennedy tried to do the same, but her boot was still pinned.

"Here." The man handed her the flashlight, reached across Willow, and tried to set her free. After a minute of struggling, Kennedy finally had to slip her foot out of its boot and edge her leg loose that way. "You'll be cold, but at least my truck's heated. It's the best we can do. Want me to carry you, or do you think you can hop?"

Kennedy tried to wiggle her toes. How long did she have before she had to worry about frostbite? She didn't even know how much time had passed since the crash. Two minutes? Twenty?

When she was outside the car, she could see the damage. The entire hood was collapsed in on itself.

"I think you're far enough to the side of the road that we don't have to worry, but I've got a few flares I'll set out just in case. I'm Roger, by the way."

With Willow supporting her on one side, Kennedy hopped toward his truck. She turned around to get one last glimpse at the damage, but Willow grabbed her more tightly. "Don't look back there. It's not pretty."

Kennedy, still somewhat dazed, soon realized that Willow had been talking about the moose and not the car.

"Told you not to look," Willow said.

Kennedy shivered.

Roger's truck was just a small two-seater, so the two girls squished together, trying to conserve heat. "Here, bend your leg so I can sit on your foot." Willow's suggestion sounded odd, but soon Kennedy could feel the painful throbbing of her pulse in her toes. At least her blood was flowing again.

Willow wrapped both arms around Kennedy. "You ok? You're shaking."

Kennedy nodded, but her teeth were chattering so hard it was difficult to speak.

"All right." Roger hopped into the driver's side with an authoritative air. "My cabin's up this way. Hold on tight. It's a bumpy road."

Calling the path through the woods a road was quite an embellishment, as Kennedy was reminded each time they bounced over whatever boulders or tree roots or potholes lay underneath the snow. She was grateful for Willow's warmth next to her, thankful that the only pain she felt was in her joints, her neck, and her throbbing foot. Relief coursed through her, but she still couldn't stop shivering.

"It's all right," Willow whispered in her ear. "We'll be there soon."

"Yup," Roger confirmed. "Cabin's just up this way."

Declaring Roger's shelter a cabin, at least in Kennedy's opinion, was even more euphemistic. Willow, who apparently had seen plenty of hand-built lodgings that were hardly bigger than a bathroom stall, seemed quite at home.

"Sorry, ladies. I'm off the grid here," Roger explained as he shined the flashlight into the dark room. "Give me a few minutes to get the generator running."

"Right on." Willow nodded as if there was nothing out of the ordinary about a bearded man who lived miles off the highway without electricity or running water or even an indoor bathroom.

While Roger stepped out, Willow seated Kennedy on a wide stump in the middle of the room and knelt in front of her. She rubbed her socked foot until the friction made it burn and asked, "You doing all right?"

Kennedy nodded, convinced that normal people didn't live out here in the middle of the wilderness with nothing but a few stacked logs and a wood stove protecting them from the negative thirty- or forty-degree temperatures that were common to Alaskan winters.

"We're going to be all right," Willow told her. "The most important thing is to get you warmed up."

No, the most important thing was to call someone they knew and tell them where they were. She looked around the small room. "Think he's got a phone?"

"There's no reception out here." Willow was still rubbing her foot vigorously.

"I know, but we need to let someone know where we are. We can't spend the night here without cell coverage or electricity or anything."

If the thought that they were trapped in a cabin with a complete stranger bothered Willow, she didn't show it. "He's got a generator."

Willow could have said he had a thermonuclear reactor for all the difference it made. What did Kennedy know about generators? What did she know about surviving with nothing but a wood stove in the middle of the Arctic? She glanced at a pile of blankets on the floor. That couldn't be his bed, could it? He'd freeze right to the ground. There was a shelf in the corner with some canned goods, mostly spam and corn and hash. Not even enough to last a week. Who was Roger and what was he doing living way out here in the middle of nowhere? Off the grid? What did that even mean? Was he hiding from the government? Maybe he was a fugitive. They should have never gotten in the truck with him, especially in a no-coverage zone.

Roger stepped back into the cabin, and Kennedy studied him as earnestly as she'd prepared for the MCATs. She wasn't sure what she was looking for exactly, bloodstains on his flannel shirt, fangs instead of yellow teeth, something sinister behind the bushy, tangled beard that would make Nick's dreadlocks look well-groomed in comparison.

"Got the power up and running," he announced.

At this proclamation, Kennedy expected Roger to flip on a light switch, but after checking each wall, she realized there were none. She glanced over at Willow, hoping to steal a pinch of her roommate's calm.

Roger adjusted some dials on a small box tucked away in the corner. Kennedy tried to guess his age. Thirty-five? Sixty? There was no way to know with his entire face covered by that ridiculous beard. It was so ratted she couldn't tell if it was more gray or brown. He wasn't young or old, skinny or overweight, the kind of person she might have walked past in the airport or movie theater and never noticed. There was nothing to learn about him from his clothing either. Flannel and jeans in Alaska were about as common as premed students in the Harvard library.

Roger pushed a button, and Kennedy flinched at the sound. She hoped he hadn't noticed, but he straightened up and stared hard at her. "Space heater," he explained. "Nothing to worry about."

Great. *Nothing to worry about.* Isn't that about like a sleazy salesman crooning *you can trust me?*

Kennedy tried to dissolve her fears in the warmth from Roger's small heating unit. At least her foot felt better now, thanks to Willow's vigorous massage.

"Where you girls from?"

"We came in from Anchorage," Willow answered while Kennedy tried sending out telepathic messages to her roommate to keep her mouth shut. Maybe it was her dad and all his paranoia, or maybe she just couldn't trust a man who actually chose to live out here in the middle of winter in nothing but a hundred-square-foot shack, but she certainly didn't want to give Roger any more information than was absolutely vital. "My parents live out in Copper Lake," Willow added, "just past Glennallen."

So much for discretion.

Roger nodded. "Pretty place."

"Oh, I know. It's gorgeous. I'm getting married there the

day after tomorrow." She sighed. "Actually, technically it's tomorrow already. Nick's going to be really worried about us. Frankenstein. I wish I could get a hold of him."

If Roger was surprised by her odd choice in exclamations, he didn't show it. "I took a look at that car of yours. Totally busted."

Kennedy waited for the part when he offered to drive them out toward Glennallen, but all he did was stare.

"You got any way to get in touch with my family?" Willow wound a strand of hair around her finger. "They're going to be wicked worried. You heard what happened earlier, didn't you?"

Roger nodded, then walked over by his small stash of food and slowly opened up a can of spam. Ignoring Willow's question, he held out the container. "I could heat it up for you, but it takes a while on the stovetop. You girls think you can handle it straight up?"

For the first time, Willow looked as terrified as Kennedy felt. "No thanks. I'm vegan."

"You're what?" Roger narrowed his eyebrows.

"Vegan," Willow repeated. "Kind of like vegetarian. I don't eat meat."

He frowned at her with suspicion then looked at Kennedy. "Do you?"

She nodded, and before she could tell him she wasn't all that hungry, he'd dumped the slab of spam into the palm of her hand. She'd never eaten it before and wasn't even sure what to do with it. She glanced at Willow, who scrunched up her face.

Roger was staring at her, so she forced herself to take the daintiest of bites. With all the salt and grease, she couldn't taste the meat itself, if it actually was meat. Kennedy wasn't sure, and Roger was still holding the can, so she couldn't read the label.

"How is it?" Willow was trying to hide a bemused smirk.

"It's ok." Kennedy forced herself to take one more taste and then looked for a place to put the rest down. Finally, Roger held out his palm. Kennedy handed him the cube of meat product, and he took a huge, noisy bite.

He pointed to the pile of blankets on the floor. "You two can curl up by the heater down there and get warm."

He didn't have any indoor plumbing or running water, and he didn't seem like the type to worry about carrying his dirty linen out to the lake every week. Besides, it would be frozen five or six months out of the year, and the closest laundromat was probably a hundred miles away. Just how dirty were those blankets? And was any amount of warmth worth risking fleas or ticks or heaven knew what else might be down here?

"Come on." Willow plopped down onto the pile and beckoned for Kennedy. "We may as well get comfortable while we wait for ..." She stopped and looked at Roger. "What exactly are we waiting for? What's the plan?"

"My buddy Buster," he answered with his mouth full of spam.

Kennedy hadn't realized there really were people named Buster in the world. She'd previously thought it was just a name you called someone you didn't like if you were a character in an old-fashioned cartoon episode.

Roger was still chewing on his canned meat. "Lives about fifteen miles down the road. Has a landline."

"Right on." Willow snuggled down in the corner of the cabin, completely unfazed.

Kennedy didn't bother to point out that even if this Buster guy had a landline phone, it did them precious little good if he was fifteen miles *down the road*, especially if Roger was referring to the little mountain trail they'd driven on to get here. Things didn't make much more sense when he took a large electronic box off the shelf.

"Buster?" He held it close to his mouth. "You hear me? Wake up, cranky."

The radio crackled, and an angry voice responded,

"What you want?"

"Got me two girls here." Roger looked them both over. "Ran into some car trouble on the Glenn, and they have to get a message home."

More static, followed by, "Oh, yeah? They all right?"

Kennedy couldn't figure out why Roger was staring at her so intensely. "Yeah. Both fine. But there's a family around Glennallen they're trying to get a hold of. If I give you a phone number, could you call them for us?" He stared at Willow. "Ready?"

He brought the radio toward her, and Willow gave Buster her parents' phone number and a message that she and Kennedy were safe but the car was totaled.

"What about someone coming to pick us up?" Kennedy asked, still unwilling to sit down next to Willow on that dirty pile of tattered blankets. She tried to figure out how far away they were from Copper Lake, how long they'd have to stay here until they were rescued. At least she wasn't as cold anymore. The space heater and stove were far more efficient than she'd initially expected.

Roger overheard Kennedy's question and grabbed the radio back. "Buster, tell her folks to come get them tomorrow morning. I'll drop them off at Eureka Lodge."

A lodge? Kennedy's brain sprang to attention at the

word. A lodge within driving distance? A lodge meant real walls, not logs piled up onto each other by hand. Heat that came out of floorboards, not a stove or space heater. Real beds, real sheets, and blankets that were at least occasionally washed by machine. Why weren't they already on their way?

"We could leave now," she suggested, but Roger was listening to his friend on the radio.

"You sure they're all right?" Buster had a wheeze in his voice. "Sound pretty young."

Roger glanced at them again. "Yeah, they're fine. Just make sure you pass their message on, got it?"

"Roger that, Roger."

"Hilarious," he grumbled. "All right, so we'll see you there."

Roger ended the call, and Kennedy wondered about his last words. *We'll see you there.* What did that mean? Did Buster live at this lodge? He had a landline, so he had to be a little closer to civilization. She still couldn't believe people voluntarily lived out here like this. Were there other mountain men, dozens of hermits like Roger, scattered through these woods?

Roger set the radio back on the top shelf and looked at Kennedy. "May as well get some rest," he told her. "I'll drive you up to Eureka in the morning."

Kennedy realized they hadn't set a time to tell Willow's parents to meet them at the lodge. What if Roger's idea of morning was 11:30, and the Winters showed up at six, frantic and worried? What if there was more than one lodge in Eureka, wherever that was? How would they find each other?

Willow motioned for Kennedy to sit down by her. "Come on," she coaxed, "you need some rest."

Kennedy couldn't argue with her. At least maybe the cold was enough to kill off bed bugs and ticks that might be living in the rags.

She hoped so as she sat down next to her roommate.

Willow started rubbing her back. "It's going to be fine," she whispered.

Kennedy scooted closer. "You think we can trust him?"

Willow smiled. "Yeah. Never mind what his home looks like. There are people like this all over the state. They're totally harmless. Don't worry about a thing."

CHAPTER 4

4:13 pm, the day before the Winter Solstice

The plane landed with a jerk and then a roar that nearly deadened Kennedy's senses. Just a few minutes after four, but the sun had already set. She didn't know if her brain was playing tricks on her or not, but she shivered with cold when she looked out at the snow piled up on the sides of the runway.

She couldn't wait to get off this plane. She'd been either in the air or waiting in some terminal for the past fourteen hours.

"You have someone here to pick you up?" the woman sitting next to her asked. They hadn't talked much on the flight, only enough for Kennedy to know she was here visiting a new grandbaby.

Kennedy nodded. "My roommate's coming."

The grandmother smiled. "Well, tell her I hope it's a

beautiful wedding."

"I will. And congrats on your daughter's baby. I hope you have a great visit."

It was almost heavenly standing up and stretching her legs once the slow deboarding process began. After traveling back and forth from China so often, Kennedy was still surprised at how much the simple four-hour time difference between Alaska and the East Coast could throw her off. Maybe the winter darkness had something to do with it. Her phone told her it was the middle of the afternoon, but her appetite was convinced it was past dinnertime and the sky was as dark as midnight.

She shifted her bookbag, which was lighter than normal since she was finally trying to get her eyes used to an e-reader. She could never fully give up on print, but it was convenient not having to lug around ten or twelve paperbacks whenever she traveled. In addition to studying up for her MCATs, she was reading as many books as she could about Alaska. Memoirs about kids who grew up in the homesteading generation like Willow's mom, photographs from the Klondike gold rush and Kennicott copper mines, collections of Native Alaskan mythology, historical fiction from the time of the Russian colonization.

Her legs were stiff from inactivity when she made her

way down the tarmac and into the Anchorage airport. Or the Ted Stevens airport, as everyone here called it. Whoever he was. She'd have to ask Willow. Kennedy had only recently realized how much unique culture was packed into this arctic state. Willow teased her mercilessly about her general lack of Alaskan knowledge, which is why Kennedy was finally studying up on its people and history.

"Excuse me, Miss."

She turned around at the nasally voice. A tall young man, awkwardly skinny and long-limbed, rushed to catch up to her.

"Hi. I'm Melvin." He held out his hand. "I couldn't help but notice you reading on the plane. Do you like books?"

Kennedy was in no mood to enter into some random conversation with a stranger. She wanted to collect her suitcase, find Willow, and crash at their hotel.

He reached into his computer bag that was strapped across his shoulder. "I was thinking, if this is the kind of reading you enjoy, I've got an extra copy back home and wondered if maybe you wanted mine."

She glanced at the cover. *Why the World Will End on the Winter Solstice.* Not a very original title, but at least it made it quite clear what the short paperback was about.

"That's ok," she said. "You should keep it."

Melvin shoved the book into her hands. "No, take it. I mean it. You'll want to be prepared." He glanced at his watch. "It's all starting soon."

Kennedy took the book in hopes that it would get him to leave her alone.

Unfortunately, she was not so lucky.

"You know about the volcano, right?" he asked as they stopped in front of the baggage claim area.

"A little bit," she answered. As if her dad hadn't called her thirteen times in the past two days to warn her. Seismological reports suggested that one of the mountains on the opposite side of the Cook Inlet was about to blow. It wasn't in an inhabited area, but the ash was supposed to cover Anchorage within an hour or two of the eruption.

"Well, that's just the start." Melvin grabbed the book out of Kennedy's hands. After turning to the second chapter, he pointed to a constellation map as the suitcases began their descent down the conveyer belt. "See? It's got all you need to know. You ever read the book of Revelation?"

Kennedy nodded.

Melvin's eyes widened. "Really? Oh, well, ok then. You've heard all about it."

"All about what?" She was glad when her suitcase came into view. That was one perk of flying into an airport as small as this one.

"About the sign in the sky, the great wonder. Revelation 12. Here." He flipped ahead a few pages. "*A great sign appeared in heaven: a woman clothed with the sun, with the moon under her feet and a crown of twelve stars on her head.* You can read all about it. Where it talks about how these astrological symbols are lining up, just like the verse says, the crown of twelve stars, everything. And it all starts tomorrow on the solstice. That's what I mean when I said you've got to be prepared."

Kennedy did her best to fake a smile. "Well, thanks for sharing. That's really ..." She cleared her throat. "That's really interesting." Grabbing her phone from her pocket, she added in what she hoped sounded like a disappointed voice, "Oh, that's my friend. She's waiting for me outside. I don't want to be late."

Without waiting for a good-bye, she grabbed her suitcase, braced herself for the biting cold, and headed into the winter darkness.

CHAPTER 5

Past midnight, Winter Solstice

There was no way that Kennedy could manage to fall asleep, even as exhausted as she felt. She'd left her cell in the totaled car and there were no clocks anywhere, but it felt like she'd been at Roger's for hours by the time he mumbled something about stepping outside for a few minutes. Kennedy was relieved when he left. Maybe Willow had seen hermits like him her entire life, but Kennedy had no idea people still lived like this in America in the twenty-first century.

She nudged her roommate who lay beside her. "You still awake?"

Willow rolled over. "Yeah. What's going on?" She sat up and arched her back.

"Roger just stepped out. Didn't say where he was going."

"Probably to use the outhouse," she answered. "You

should try to sleep. It's late."

"I don't like this place." Kennedy kept her voice low in case Roger was close by. "Gives me the creeps."

Willow shrugged. "Early days, everyone lived like this. Little cabins, you see them all over the place. My grandpa built one just like it. It's pretty standard for the homestead generation. You make yourself a quick cabin in the spring, clear the land and get your crops planted, and then after you get ahead a little you make yourself a proper home. My grandparents lived in a one-room like this until my mom was two or three. It's still there on the property. Remind me to show you."

Kennedy didn't reply. She was too busy trying to guess how much longer it'd be until morning. "Do you have your phone?" she asked Willow.

"Yeah, but there's no reception out here."

"I know. I was just wondering what time it was."

Willow glanced out the tiny window by Roger's cupboard. "Probably right after one." She pulled out her phone to check. "Yup. It's 1:13."

"How'd you do that?"

Willow shrugged. "Just looked at the angle of the moon. It's not neuroscience."

It was times like these that made Kennedy realize how

ignorant she was about rural living. Even on their busy campus in Cambridge, Willow was always commenting about the lunar phases, telling Kennedy when a harvest moon was due or when a meteor shower was passing through.

"I wish it weren't so dark in here," Kennedy said.

Willow tapped her screen. "Hold on. I can turn this thing into a flashlight."

The cabin was no less creepy now than it had been in the dark.

"I can't wait until we get out of this place."

Willow reached over and offered a reassuring squeeze. "We'll be fine. If it weren't for me worrying about getting back home, I'd actually be enjoying our little adventure."

"What about that Eureka place?" Kennedy asked.

"It's not that far. Maybe twenty minutes' drive. Roger'll take us there in the morning. They've got decent food too. No more spam for breakfast."

Kennedy tried to match her smile.

"Don't worry," Willow said. "Just think about all we have to be thankful for. If your plane had come a few hours later, you might not have been able to land at all. We got out of Anchorage in plenty of time, and that moose could have done a lot more damage than it did. Honestly, it's a miracle

Roger found us. We could have been lying in that car for hours before somebody drove by. This is all just part of being in Alaska, really. You have to learn to be flexible." She chuckled. "And you have to learn to watch the road for moose."

Kennedy let out her breath. "There's still something really off about this place."

"You're just not used to roughing it, City Girl."

Maybe Willow was right. Maybe Kennedy needed to be more flexible. More adventurous like her roommate.

Or maybe she just needed to be at that lodge in Eureka, sleeping in a real bed and not on a pile of rags.

"You want proof that there's nothing here to worry about?" Willow stood and shined her phone light around. "I'm telling you, I know all about these little homestead cabins. See, over here, this is where he keeps his two coffee mugs, two tin plates, fork, knife, and a spoon." She pulled open a drawer. "Oh, look. I was wrong. He actually has two spoons." She held them up.

"And over here, you've already seen his pantry. Spam, canned corn, and Ramen. Hey, just like Nick eats. And this ..." She picked up a shoebox. "I bet this is where he keeps every single personal item he owns." She paused with her hand on the lid. "Wait, let me guess. An expired driver's license, a postcard from his mom or grandma, and a third-grade report card." She opened the box with a grand gesture.

"We shouldn't be going through his stuff." Kennedy glanced nervously at the door. If Roger was just using the outhouse, he'd be back any second.

"I want to prove to you that this man is totally harmless. Like I said, he ..." Willow froze.

So did the blood in Kennedy's veins. "What? What is it?"

"Dude." Willow shook her head.

"What?" Kennedy repeated. "If this is your idea of a joke ..."

Headlights shined in through the window. Willow threw on the lid, shoved the box back on the shelf, and all but dove into Kennedy's lap.

"What's the matter?" Kennedy hissed.

"Just lie down," Willow whispered. "Lie down and pretend to be asleep." She thrust her cell phone into Kennedy's hand. "And the minute you get the chance, run."

CHAPTER 6

4:41 pm, the day before the Winter Solstice

"Dude, you made it!" Willow wrapped both arms around Kennedy's neck and kissed her loudly on both cheeks.

Kennedy tried to muster up the energy to return her roommate's enthusiasm. Willow had been in Alaska for almost a week, making last-minute plans and getting everything ready for her wedding. Kennedy just wanted to grab some food and take a hot shower. She hoped that whatever hotel they were staying at for the night had good water pressure. She hated the feel of grime and sweat and germs on her skin after a full day of traveling.

Kennedy hefted her suitcase into the trunk of her roommate's car and only then noticed Willow's pout.

"Well?" Willow jutted out her hip and frowned. "Aren't you going to say anything?"

Kennedy hardly looked up. "About what?"

Willow stood silent and stared until Kennedy raised her eyes.

"Woah, your hair," she exclaimed once full realization set in. "It looks ... It's ..."

"Normal?" Willow finished for her. "Well, don't get your hopes up too high. I told Nick that as soon as we've taken the wedding pictures, the first thing I'm going to do on our honeymoon is dye it. I'm thinking of going black again. Black with gray streaks. What do you think?"

Kennedy was still staring. "So, is that your ... I mean ..."

Willow smiled. "Yeah, I'm a natural brunette. It's been so long since I've seen my real color I hardly recognize myself. At first, I was planning on doing it the same shade of red as the flowers, but then I started to think that maybe one day I'll be a respectable old church lady, and I might not want my wedding pictures to stand out so much. I don't know.

"Oh, speaking of wedding pictures, have I told you what my dad did yesterday? He surprised us, sent Nick and me on this helicopter glacier tour with a professional photographer. It was wicked cold, but I've seen one or two of the unedited pictures, and it was totally worth it. But look at you. You're freezing. Get into the car. I've kept it warming up while I waited."

Kennedy didn't argue. Classic rock music was blaring when she sank down into the passenger seat.

Willow sat beside her and smiled. "Hope you got a long nap on the plane. You're going to have to stay awake for a while."

No. Kennedy couldn't. "I thought we were going to head to the hotel and crash."

Willow snorted. "Well, there may be a few people who decide to crash, but I think everybody I know has already been invited."

Kennedy still wasn't following. "Invited to what?"

Willow raised her penciled eyebrows. "To my bachelorette party. Didn't you get my text? There'll be like forty of us, and we've got to go get ready because we only have five hours until they start showing up."

Kennedy was furiously scrolling through her phone messages.

Willow laughed. "I'm just kidding. Don't worry. There's no party."

It was a miracle that Kennedy's sigh of relief didn't blow the rainbow heart decals off Willow's dashboard.

Willow was still chuckling as they rolled away from the airport curb. "You should have seen your face!"

Kennedy did her best to share in the joke, but all she

could think about was a steamy shower. Even with Willow's heater blaring full-power, it didn't penetrate her frozen core. She glanced out the window, surprised that there was actually traffic in a city this small. "So how far do we have to go to get to the hotel?"

Willow turned her head and yelled, "What? I can't hear you."

Kennedy repeated her question.

Willow turned down the radio. "Well, we could head over there right now. We're not too far, but if you don't mind, I'd like to make a quick stop downtown first. There's this cute little museum gift shop, and I still haven't found the right centerpieces for the reception. I thought I might get some ideas there."

Kennedy didn't mention that two days before her wedding was a little bit late to be shopping for décor. But as exhausted as she was, she still wanted to try to be a help to her roommate. "Sure, sounds interesting. I didn't even know Anchorage had a downtown."

Willow mumbled something about Kennedy being a greenhorn and continued driving.

As it turned out, downtown Anchorage was nothing more than a bunch of touristy shops lining congested streets. Willow spent a full twenty minutes driving in circles, hunting for a place to parallel park without traveling the wrong direction on a one-way street. Right when Kennedy figured she was going to fall asleep, Willow found a spot. "Well," she said cheerily, "at least we're close to the museum."

Kennedy didn't want to leave the relatively warm car, but she made herself get out and stamped her feet on the snowy sidewalk to try to stay warm. Willow grabbed her by the elbow. "Come on, rookie. We'll make a real Alaska girl out of you yet." She led Kennedy into a small storefront entrance with bells on the door that clanged and jingled when they entered.

An old man with spectacles about to fall off his nose smiled at them. "Welcome to the Alaska Historical Museum. I'm Jeb. You from out of town?" he asked, staring right at Kennedy.

She nodded. "Just flew in."

He scratched his cheek. "You look colder than a tourist in July." He turned to Willow. "What about you? Where you from?"

"Born and raised in Copper Lake." There was a hint of pride in Willow's voice.

Jeb let out a low whistle. "Yeah, how cold does it get out there this time of year?"

"It was thirty-eight below when I went out this morning to milk the goats."

"You have goats?" Jeb asked. "Any babies?"

"We have two pregnant does, but they won't kid until spring."

While Willow started browsing through the Alaska trinkets and souvenirs, Kennedy walked up and down the aisles of the small one-room museum.

"That there's about the Aleutian chain during World War II," Jeb told her. "Japanese came and took over two of our islands. Only US soil they managed to claim the entire war."

Kennedy didn't even know where the Aleutians were, but she wasn't about to flaunt her ignorance.

"And there," Jeb said, "those were supplies they gave the Washtub recruits in Seward during the Cold War."

Kennedy replayed that last sentence several times in her head and still failed to decipher any of it.

Willow, apparently forgetting that she was shopping for an Alaskan centerpiece, held up a pair of beaded earrings. "Dude, these are adorable. I have to get them."

Jeb seemed much more interested in giving Kennedy a crash course in Alaskan history than in making a sale. "You see our new '64 display?" He snaked his way out from behind the counter and led Kennedy to panels of large black-

and-white photographs on the wall.

Kennedy squinted at pictures of collapsed houses, ruined railroad tracks, and massive cracks in roads and sidewalks. "What's this?"

"That's our '64 display. Didn't I just say that?"

Kennedy glanced at Willow for translation.

"The big Alaska earthquake," she explained.

Jeb looped his thumbs in his belt buckles and nodded approvingly. "Largest earthquake on record in North America."

"Were you here then?" Willow asked.

Jeb nodded. "Oh yeah. Wife and I just bought our first house in Turnagain. We had a bookshelf at the top of the hall. Darn thing chased me all the way down the stairs before crashing into the coffee table."

Kennedy had never felt an earthquake before, nor had she come across this part of Alaska's past in her reading on the airplane.

Jeb stared at the pictures on the wall. "Molly kept trying to run out the door to get to the kids. They were playing outside, but the ground was shaking so bad it just kept throwing her down. Like trying to run across a waterbed. We got out of the house as soon as it was over, and our front yard had turned into a cliff. Ten, maybe twenty-foot drop.

Thankfully the kids were safe in the backyard." He cleared his throat. "You should've heard the sound. Thought the Soviets were finally bombing us. That's how loud it was."

Kennedy didn't know what to say. Thankfully, Jeb seemed lost in his own thoughts as he stared at the photographs.

Willow came over and plopped several items on the counter. "Found what I needed." She studied her painted fingernails while Jeb rang up several new pairs of earrings, beaded moccasins, a colorfully died scarf, and a pair of men's gloves. Kennedy didn't bother to ask her about that wedding centerpiece.

"You two girls heard about the volcano warning, haven't you?" Jeb asked as he ran Willow's credit card.

Willow nodded. "Yeah, wicked crazy, huh?"

He shrugged. "Some loonies came in trying earlier to tell me to close up shop and make for the hills. Saying the solstice marks the end of the world or some nonsense like that."

Kennedy ignored the flutter in her gut and wondered if she'd done the right thing by throwing away that book the man had given her at the airport.

"So I told them," Jeb went on, "the only thing the solstice marks the end of is each day getting darker, right?" He let out a wheezy laugh. "You two girls take it easy now. Stay safe."

His words followed them out the door, sending another shiver racing down Kennedy's spine. Or maybe that was just the cold.

"I didn't know about that big earthquake," Kennedy confessed as they headed back to Willow's car.

"Yeah, it's a big deal around here. Mom was seven or eight. She had relatives living in Valdez at the time. Got a big tidal wave there. Her uncle was working the docks and disappeared. Never found his body. It was wicked intense."

Kennedy couldn't even imagine. "Have there been any other earthquakes since?"

Willow shrugged as they got into her car. "They come and go. I've lived through dozens, but none that ever caused any damage or lasted more than a few seconds. Most of the time, you don't even know it's an earthquake until it's over. The one in '64 lasted something like five minutes, and if you talk to anybody who remembers, it was terrifying. Mom still gets a little spooked by any sort of loud rumbling noise."

Kennedy focused on buckling her seatbelt and was proud that her hands didn't shake. Two years ago, when her PTSD was at its worst, this kind of conversation might have triggered a full-on panic attack. But logically she knew she had very little to worry about. People had been living safely in Alaska for decades. Even with the weird seismological occurrences on the other side of the Cook Inlet, the kind of disaster Jeb was talking about was a once in a century kind of event at most. Even if another serious earthquake was doomed to hit Alaska in the next fifty or hundred years, there was no reason to think it would happen in the next few days.

What would be the chances?

CHAPTER 7

Kennedy's phone rang a few seconds after they got back on the road.

She sighed and rolled her eyes before answering. "Hi, Dad."

"Hey, Princess. You made it in safely?"

"Yeah. Everything's fine." Could he take the hint and stop worrying about her? If it weren't for his constant paranoia, would she still struggle with anxiety as much as she did?

"Great." At least his voice was cheerful. "I've been keeping my eyes on the reports. Looks like that volcano's been pretty quiet the past ten hours or so."

Kennedy didn't know what to say in response.

"Well, just stay safe, all right?"

"I will."

Her roommate was chuckling when Kennedy ended the call.

"What's so funny?"

"Your dad. Has he always been like that?"

"Yeah, but he means well."

"Oh, I know he does. That man would seriously do anything to keep you safe. It's wicked cute."

Cute isn't the word Kennedy would have chosen, but she decided not to argue.

"So what's he think about the whole winter solstice, end of the world thing? Does he buy into that?"

Kennedy shook her head. "No. I mean, there's been some weird stuff going on lately, those typhoons and tornados and things. And obviously he's convinced that the volcano's going to erupt and bury us in ash. But more than anything, I think he's worried people might start acting crazy. Like riots are about to break out all over Anchorage." Kennedy chuckled, but surprisingly Willow didn't share her laugh.

"A lot of people are worried about that."

Kennedy glanced over to try to tell if she was joking.

"Anchorage might not be that big of a city, but crime is awful here. It's got one of the highest per capita murder rates in the nation. Same thing with rape. It's terrible."

Kennedy had no idea.

"Some of it has to do with the gangs in the Lower 48.

The jails get so full they pay to relocate criminals up here. Just set them free in Anchorage. I would never want to live in a city like this."

"I wouldn't have guessed."

Willow shrugged. "Most people wouldn't. They think Alaska's all frontiersmen and fishing and igloos, but there's a major poverty and crime problem here. It's something Nick and I have talked about. We still aren't sure where God's calling us after we get married because there are so many needs everywhere. That's why we agreed for me to take the semester off, spend that time praying to find out what he wants us to do."

Kennedy wasn't ready to think about returning to college next semester without her roommate. "How long will you be with Nick's family in Washington?" she asked.

"Oh!" Willow swerved so fast that Kennedy thought they were about to crash.

"What was that?" Kennedy snapped her head back, checking the road for signs of danger.

"I just missed our turn." Crossing two more lanes of traffic, Willow backtracked down a somewhat shady-looking side street.

"This is where we're staying tonight?" Kennedy hoped her voice didn't give away her concern.

"No, silly." Willow pulled the car into a crowded lot. "This is where we're having dinner. Welcome to the Raven's Claw, home of the best pizza in Alaska. Or anywhere else for that matter."

Once inside the restaurant, Kennedy doubted that even the most delicious pizza in the universe could warrant a ninety-minute wait. After three and a half games of smart phone Scrabble and another forty minutes from the time they ordered until their food arrived at the table, Kennedy would have been willing to eat roadkill moose or fried whale blubber.

Fortunately, the food was just as good as Willow had promised, even their vegan pizza made with cheese alternative. They finished dinner with nothing left over. "Come on." Willow grabbed Kennedy's hand after they'd paid the bill. "If we hurry, we'll make it on time."

"Make it where?" As far as Kennedy knew, the only thing she had to make tonight was her hotel room bed.

"There's that new movie out. Remember? The Christian flick about the end times. I haven't been to the theater in months, and I'm really curious about this one." Willow unlocked the car door and got in. "You know, I read all of Revelations. I even wrote down my questions to ask Pastor Carl, but he's so busy with church and still gets those bad headaches after his accident, and I hate to bother him. So what I was thinking was we can go see the movie tonight, and on the drive home tomorrow, we can go through the list because I know some of them are really basic. If you could answer those, then I wouldn't have to feel guilty for wasting Pastor Carl's time later on."

"It's getting pretty late," Kennedy began tentatively.

"Oh, don't worry about that. The theater's right around the corner."

"I'm not sure I'll be able to stay awake."

Willow smiled. "I know. I've heard it's super cheesy, and we'll probably get a lot of good laughs, but I'm still curious about it. Especially with what everyone's saying about the winter solstice and those constellations lining up like in that prophecy."

Kennedy had read the book the movie was based on years ago. It was an engaging story, but she wasn't sure how useful it would be for helping Willow understand Revelation, at least not without someone like Carl to help her make sense of what was biblical and what was fiction.

Thankfully, last fall Carl had astounded his doctors when he woke up from his coma, but he got tired more easily and sometimes suffered such debilitating migraines he had to take a day or two off work. Willow was right about one thing. If Kennedy could help get some of her questions answered, it would give Carl more time to rest and focus on his family and his preaching and his recovery.

The problem was Kennedy had no clue what she thought about the end times. The only solid opinion she had on the matter was that she hoped to be buried and dead long before any of the events in Revelation started to unfold.

"Why don't you ask Nick?" she asked.

Willow strummed her fingers on the steering wheel in time with the music on her radio. "Oh, you know Nick," she sighed. "I love that man to death, but when he starts talking theology, you better have a master's degree if you want to keep up with him. Which is probably why he and my dad get along so well."

Kennedy didn't have time to come up with any better plans before Willow pulled her car up alongside a miniature trailer in an empty parking lot. "Come on. I'll get you a coffee. That way you'll be able to stay awake."

"I'm really not sure …"

Willow nudged Kennedy playfully. "Stop being so uptight. You don't have any classes to get up early for tomorrow. It will be fun."

CHAPTER 8

Kennedy had never seen a drive-up coffee hut like this before, but Willow told her they were all over the state. "I read online that if you took every stand in Alaska and stacked them from one point to the other, they would stretch all the way from Anchorage to Santa Barbara."

Kennedy wasn't so sure about that, but she could at least appreciate the convenience of grabbing a hot drink without having to get out of the car. Willow rolled down her window long enough to give her order then shut it again to keep out the cold.

Kennedy was surprised to see the girl inside was wearing nothing but tight shorts and a tank top. "She must be freezing."

"Don't worry, she's probably got a couple space heaters in there. I'm sure she's perfectly toasty."

Kennedy tried not to stare while the young girl mixed their drinks.

Willow raised her eyebrows at her. "Sheesh. Haven't you heard of a bikini barista before? They're all over Anchorage. That's why these coffee stands make such good money."

"So they get paid to look pretty in their swimsuits?"

"No, they get paid to make coffee. They get tips for looking pretty in their swimsuits."

Willow was joking, but Kennedy didn't think it was all that funny. "Isn't that dangerous? I mean, it's the middle of the night, totally dark. She's out here all alone ..."

Willow laughed. "First of all, that's a perfect example of rape culture right there. Second, she's an Alaska chick. Probably packs more heat than that police detective back in Boston. Don't be so uptight. In the past five years, there's only been one barista kidnapping."

"Only one?" Kennedy repeated sarcastically.

"Really sad story, actually. She grew up in Valdez, girl named Brandy. We knew each other from a few summer theater programs. Anyway, don't worry, she didn't even work at one of the bikini ones."

Willow rolled down her window to grab the two drinks. Kennedy kept her eyes on the dashboard.

"Oh, stop being all weird about it," Willow said as they drove off. "That barista's probably a straight-A student like you, working one or two late nights a week and earning enough in tips to pay for her entire college education."

They arrived at the theater two minutes before starting time. As they hurried through the parking lot, the air stung Kennedy's face, and she wondered how she'd handle Copper Lake, which was regularly thirty degrees colder or more than Anchorage.

Kennedy had never seen her roommate get so engrossed in a film before, especially not one with such canned dialogue and stiff acting as this one. Forty minutes into the movie, Kennedy found herself nodding off as many times as the camera changed its angle. She shouldn't have gotten a plain hot chocolate at the drive-up stand, not if her goal was to stay awake. She should either stop fighting her fatigue and squeeze in an hour-long nap or run out to the lobby and grab herself something more caffeinated. It didn't matter which she chose. Either option would be preferable to sitting here jerking herself awake every two or three minutes.

The main character was explaining the rapture to the perky love interest when Kennedy leaned over and whispered to Willow, "I'm going to grab a drink. Be right back."

Not surprisingly, the theater was almost empty. Kennedy didn't have to worry about stepping over anybody's legs or distracting any viewers behind her.

She stopped by the bathroom on the way to the concession stand and splashed cold water on her face. She could travel across twelve time zones a couple times a year and manage not to turn into a zombie. With a little gumption and a whole lot of caffeine, she could make it through the rest of this film.

She stared at her reflection, wondering what strangers thought when they saw her. She wasn't like Willow, never was one to stand out in a crowd. Not that she wanted to. She thought back to her first international flight by herself two and a half years ago. Straight out of high school, never suspecting the trials she'd have to walk through. She still didn't feel all that old, but she was definitely more mature than she'd been when she first stepped foot on the campus of Harvard University.

The same university that last semester had humiliated her, taken away her job as a teaching assistant, and threatened her medical school acceptance when all she'd done was write an article that certain people didn't like. She might have never gotten her offer reinstated if it hadn't been for her friend, Ian. The red-haired journalist had championed tirelessly for her before hopping on a plane to China to continue with his filming.

She hadn't heard from him since, which shouldn't

disappoint her all that much. They'd only had a few breakfast dates together, not enough to know if there really was any spark or chemistry between them. Still, she'd thought he would at least text or email her from overseas, even just to let her know he was still safe.

She sighed as she made her way out of the bathroom. Standing in line to get a drink, she felt her pocket vibrate and realized she'd missed several texts from her dad during the first portion of the film.

Her mouth immediately went dry. She could taste the fear in the back of her throat. Her lungs constricted once. She did her best to swallow down her panic.

There wasn't time to write her dad back. Praying Willow had forgotten to turn her phone off before the start of the show, she steadied her hands enough to send a simple text.

Volcano erupted about twenty minutes ago. We've got to leave.

CHAPTER 9

Past midnight, Winter Solstice

Kennedy winced as Willow's fingernails dug into her arm. She wanted to ask what was going on, what Willow had found in the box that got her so freaked out, but she was paralyzed.

"Roger? You home?" The front door banged opened, bringing in with it a burst of cold and the foul smell of body odor.

Willow gave Kennedy's arm one last squeeze and asked sleepily, "Someone there?"

"I'm looking for Roger. Where is he?" The voice was gruff.

"He stepped out for just a sec. I'm sure he'll be back soon. Are you Buster, the guy with the radio?"

"Yeah, that's me. Who're you?"

"I'm Willow. Did you get hold of my parents?"

"Sure did. They were pretty worried, too."

"Oh, good. Thank you so much for getting that message to them. Hey, did my mom mention my goat?"

"Goat?"

Willow's voice was laced with concern. She sounded five years younger. "Yeah, she went into labor this morning, and I've been really worried about her. I thought for sure my mom would know how scared I'd be and give you a message to let me know how things went."

Buster cleared his throat. "Oh, that. Yeah, she said everything went just fine. No problems. Happy mama, healthy baby."

Willow let out her breath in a loud sigh. "I'm so glad. I've been worried sick."

Kennedy couldn't keep ahead of the conversation. What was Willow talking about?

Buster's voice softened a little. He scratched his massive belly. "Where's your friend? Roger said there were two of you here."

Willow let out an airy laugh that held no indication of how tightly she'd been squeezing Kennedy's arm just a minute earlier. "She's dead to the world. That's her way. She's like Cinderella. Turns into a pumpkin after midnight, or something like that." Another giggle.

Buster cleared his throat. "Roger say when he was coming back?"

"No. Should we sit and wait for him?" Something in Willow's voice had changed. She wasn't actually flirting with this mountain man, was she?

Buster lowered his weight onto the stump in the middle of the room. Now that he was closer to Kennedy's corner, she tried hard not to gag from the smell.

"Is it still pretty cold out?" Willow asked. What kind of question was that? It was the dead of winter, and they were stuck here freezing in the middle of nowhere.

"You could say that."

"I wonder if the stars are out. Want to step outside and see?" What was Willow thinking? Why would she go outside in the cold with this stranger? Kennedy thought about her roommate's directive to run when she got the chance, but she wasn't going anywhere by herself. Not without Willow, and not without a whole lot more answers.

What had Willow seen? What got her so scared? They were obviously in some kind of trouble, but until Kennedy knew what, until she found out what was in that box that spooked Willow so much, she had to be prepared for anything. What was lying around here that could make a decent weapon? There was a fire poker, wasn't there? Which side of the stove was it on? Kennedy reached out her hand slowly, terrified of making any noise that would alert Buster and let him know she was awake.

"Come on," Willow was coaxing playfully. "Take me outside so we can look at the sky. Don't you love the stars?" She sounded like an eight-year-old begging for a ride on the merry-go-round.

"You can see the sky and the stars from here. Just look right out the window. Don't even have to get cold."

"Yeah, but there's a spot right behind the house that I bet has an even better view. See that tree branch? It's blocking the view."

Buster made some sort of indecipherable grumble.

"Please?" Willow whined.

Think. Kennedy had to think. Figure out what she was supposed to do.

"Come on, let's go look. Just for a minute. We'll go behind the cabin, see if the view's better without the tree blocking it, and then we'll come right back in and warm up. Ok?"

Buster continued to speak in grunts and monosyllables, but since he was getting up off the log, Kennedy guessed he was assenting. Now was the time to make her decision.

Willow giggled. "Just behind the cabin," she repeated, glancing back once, "and then we'll come back real quick."

The door opened. The burst of searing cold nearly stole Kennedy's breath. As soon as she was alone she jumped up to grab the shoebox from the shelf. She had to understand what Willow was doing. Why she'd told Kennedy to run.

She shined the light from Willow's phone into the box. An old faded newspaper clipping lay on the top. *Anchorage Barista Still Missing: Police urge anyone with information to come forward.* Beneath the headline, a girl in a tank top smiled at Kennedy.

She moved the clipping aside. Beneath it were piles of photographs of a young woman in lingerie. Kennedy was certain that even from outside Buster and Willow could hear her pounding heart.

It was the same girl from the newspaper article.

She had to get Willow out of there. That was all there was to it. Even if Willow had made the sacrificial decision to distract Buster behind the cabin so Kennedy could make her escape, there was no way she was leaving here by herself.

She grabbed the fire poker then ran to the kitchen drawer, hoping to find something sharper than a butter knife. She shoved Willow's phone in her pocket. Stupid cell phone reception.

She eyed the radio. If she could figure out how it worked, would there be a way to signal for help? Would there be time?

"Buster? That you?"

Kennedy froze. It was Roger. She had no idea where he'd gone for so long, but his truck hadn't moved. Wherever he'd been, he'd gotten there by foot.

"It's me," Buster said. "Your cute little houseguest here wanted to see the stars."

Kennedy didn't have time to think about the girl in the pictures in Roger's shoebox. The front door opened, startling Kennedy so much she dropped the fire poker, which clattered on the hard floor, stinging her ears through the silence of the winter night.

"Everything ok?" Roger asked. Was he suspicious?

Kennedy wished she could absorb her roommate's acting abilities. She forced a smile. "Yeah, I don't know much about these wood stoves, but I was feeling a little cold in here, so I was ..."

Buster came in behind Roger, leading Willow who gave Kennedy a small shake of the head.

Kennedy stared at her feet. "I'm sorry. I probably should have left it alone."

Roger let out a laugh. He seemed far more jocular than he'd been earlier. Maybe the pack of beer he was holding with two cans missing explained why.

"Shut the door." Roger slammed the cans down. It took up his entire counter space. "I hope you girls got a little rest. Buster and me were thinking we'd treat you to an early Christmas party."

Kennedy was trying to find a way to politely decline when Willow sidled up beside her and grabbed her by the wrist. "Actually, I'm dying for a drink, but can you show us where the outhouse is first?" She shot her radiant smile. "We girls like to freshen up before a good party, right?"

Buster, all 250 stench-infested pounds of him, was leaning over Willow, grinning so widely Kennedy was surprised there wasn't already a puddle of drool on her roommate's shoulder.

Roger furrowed his brow. "I'll show you where it is, but there's not room for both of you at once."

Willow gave Kennedy a very obvious nudge. "Sounds good. You go first."

Kennedy understood what Willow was trying to do but refused to leave her roommate here alone. "That's ok. I can wait." She winced when Willow's fingernails dug into her wrist.

Willow sighed but kept her voice cheerful when she said, "All right, then. I guess we'll use the outhouse later. Who's ready to get this party started?

CHAPTER 10

If Kennedy had her choice, the last thing she'd want to see would be these two men drunk, but Willow kept on giggling and popping lids off their beer. Kennedy held her full can close to her body as if it might ward off leering eyes, reminding herself to raise it to her lips every few minutes so it looked like she was taking a drink. Willow, by contrast, was already on her second can and was acting even more boisterous than she'd been back in her former partying days.

The twelve-pack was gone by the time Willow put her hand on Buster's shoulder and said, "You must be getting really tired. Think we should call it a night?" She glanced at Kennedy, who tried to guess what her roommate was thinking.

Trust me.

It wasn't Willow's voice she heard, even though she could sense that's what her gaze was meant to convey.

Trust me.

Her heart was pounding. She'd never been the type who "heard God" like some Christians she knew. Dominic, the chaplain of the police department back in Boston, had been incredibly gifted like that. Sometimes he had called Kennedy to say something like, "Hey, I was praying about you and just felt like God was telling me to give you some encouragement." Once, they'd been on their way to have dinner at Angelo's Pizza, but Dominic had said, "You know, this is going to sound crazy, but I really feel like the Lord's telling me we should go somewhere else tonight." So they grabbed clam chowder served in sourdough bread rolls from a walk-up stand, only to find out several hours later there'd been a gunfight right across the street from Angelo's.

Trust me.

Was that voice really God's? How could Kennedy be sure?

Roger's hand was on her shoulder. His breath stank and was hot on her neck. "You didn't drink much." He glanced at her beer, which Willow quickly grabbed.

"Let me take your empty can off your hands." She set it on the counter and smiled at Buster. "So, what happens now?"

Kennedy didn't understand why Willow was acting so friendly and eager, but she also couldn't shake that voice she'd heard.

Trust me.

Buster groaned as he plopped onto the tree log and pulled Willow onto his lap with a slurred, "Come here, you."

Willow giggled, but her serious eyes were fixed on Kennedy. What was she trying to say?

Trust me.

Kennedy took a deep breath. Tried not to shudder when Roger ran his hands up the back of her shirt and onto her bare skin. Kennedy was no actor. She wasn't like Willow. She couldn't pretend that any of this was right.

Willow was staring at her. What was she supposed to do?

Roger pressed his cheek against hers, the coarse hair from his beard bristling her skin and sending goosebumps up her spine.

She had to get him off. But how? Her entire body was frozen. She couldn't find her voice.

If that had really been God telling her to trust him, why wasn't he doing anything to stop Roger? Her body shivered.

"What's wrong, baby?" he asked. "You cold?"

Kennedy tried to swallow past the shameful lump in her throat. She hated the paralysis she felt, hated the helplessness that held her captive.

She didn't have to stand there like a statue and take this

humiliation. She wouldn't. If she could just snap her brain out of its stupor, she could get him to stop. She'd force him to stop. When his hand started traveling around toward her chest, reflexes kicked in. She made her hand into a fist and slammed it into his groin. He doubled over, then reached out and grabbed her by the hair.

Willow yelled something, but Kennedy couldn't make out what was going on. It took all her focus to try to pry herself away from Roger's clutches.

"Get over here," he growled.

She lunged forward. He grabbed her by the waist. She brought her leg up, tried to kick, and missed. He was standing behind her now, taller than she was. Stronger, but she wasn't about to give up. Not without the fight of her life.

He wrapped his arms around her from behind. She snapped her head back and crashed her skull against him as hard as she could. She didn't know if she hit him in the chin or the cheek or the nose, but he swore and let go. She lunged toward the fire poker.

"I don't think so," he snarled.

There was no room to run. By the door, Willow was struggling with Buster. Even if Kennedy got herself free from Roger, there was nowhere to escape.

She thought about all that beer. Maybe they'd be too

tired to fight for long. Maybe that had been Willow's plan all along. Kennedy recalled that still, small voice from just a minute earlier.

Trust me.

Ok, God, she answered back, *I'll start trusting you the minute you get us out of here.*

Roger grabbed her sweater and was trying to tear it off. Kennedy was using everything she could think of — fingernails, fists, feet. From somewhere behind her, Willow yelped in pain.

God, get us out of here.

A rumbling. It started low and came from the ground, as if something buried far beneath the cabin floor was awakening for the first time.

Angry.

It was the distraction she needed. She grabbed the poker and when Roger lunged toward her, she swung it at his head. She hadn't meant to hit so hard. Hadn't meant to do any real damage. She just wanted him to leave her alone. He crumpled to the ground. Kennedy stared and realized the fight had made her completely dizzy. She could hardly support her weight, as if the ground itself were rocking back and forth.

And what was that loud noise?

"Earthquake!" Willow grabbed the metal bar out of Kennedy's hands and whacked Buster in his massive gut. He doubled over, still conscious, and Willow grabbed Kennedy's hand. "Let's go."

Buster was so large and the cabin so small Kennedy practically had to climb over him. Willow gave him one last hit in the back with the poker, enough to give the two girls the head start they'd need to escape.

Once outside, Kennedy stumbled in the snow. She looked up. Trees were swaying. Over the angry roar from the earth beneath her, she could hear tree trunks snapping as easily as if they were twigs.

"Watch out!" Willow dove at Kennedy and covered her body as a great spruce landed on the roof. Kennedy shrieked as the cabin folded in on itself like a house of collapsing cards.

"This way."

Kennedy could hardly make out Willow's words. She felt her pulse surging through her ears but could only hear the deafening roar. How long had it been going on already? The earth couldn't sustain that kind of violence much longer. Every single tree would collapse before it was over.

Kennedy screamed again when the ground beneath her bulged up several feet, throwing her and Willow down.

Kennedy landed with her stomach on a tree stump. Where was all the air? She couldn't inhale. She was going to faint.

No, there it was. Her breath returned to her lungs in pitiful spasms. When would it end?

She'd been following Willow blindly but realized that they were running behind the cabin now. They were going the wrong way. She reached out to grab Willow's hand, but the ground heaved and she fell again.

Willow yanked her to her feet. "Hurry."

Kennedy looked over her shoulder. "The road's back there."

Willow shook her head and pointed. In the distance was another shed, even smaller than Roger's. How had Willow known it was there, and why were they heading deeper into the woods?

A spruce tree that must have been twenty or thirty feet tall whipped down, its bare branches slapping her in the face. She tried to shield her eyes. They were almost to the shed. Willow surged ahead and threw the door open.

Kennedy recognized her immediately. The girl from the photos, the missing barista. What was she doing back here? How had Willow known? She was curled in the corner, shielding her face.

"Brandy, it's ok. We've got to get you out of here."

Willow knelt down beside her.

"I can't leave," she answered in a panic. "He'll find me."

Willow was fumbling with something by her hands. Was Brandy cuffed to the wall?

"The man who trapped you is buried under his house. It collapsed on him. You don't have any reason to be afraid anymore," Willow said as the floor rolled like ocean waves during a storm.

"I can't go. He'll be too angry."

"He's dead," Willow snapped. "Dead or close to it. And we will be too if we don't find someplace safe. Now how do we get you free?"

With wide eyes, Brandy nodded toward the wall. Kennedy grabbed the key hanging by the door but had to try several times to get it into the lock.

The cuffs fell loose.

"We've got to get out of here," Willow said. "This place will collapse any minute."

"He's going to find me," Brandy protested.

"No, he's not."

The ground was still shaking, but the rolling heaves had stopped, and they could hear more than just the angry bellows of the earth. The cabin creaked and groaned.

"Come on." Kennedy took Brandy by the hand, but she

couldn't pull her up.

"I can't. I'm not …"

When Kennedy bent down to slide her arm around her waist, she realized Brandy was pregnant. Very pregnant. She propped her up on one side, and Willow took the other.

"Can you walk?" Willow asked.

"I have to stay here," Brandy insisted. "He'll be angry."

Willow and Kennedy led her toward the door. "Let's go."

Everything stopped in an instant. At first, Kennedy thought she might have blacked out. As fast as the noise came, it was now completely silent. She was dizzy from being tossed and heaved around like a bath toy in white water rapids, but now it was only her brain that thought she was still moving.

Still inside the cabin, she looked over at Willow. "Is it over?" she asked.

"Might be for now." Willow led Brandy toward the door. "But we're definitely not out of the woods yet."

CHAPTER 11

After Willow took her sweater off and wrapped it around Brandy's shoulders, the rescued girl returned to her spot against the wall where she drew her legs up toward her pregnant belly and cowered. Willow led Kennedy to the opposite side of the cabin so they could talk about what they should do.

"I don't see how those two drunk buffoons could have survived the cabin crashing in on them, but we can't be too careful either. I'm not sure any of us are in a position to walk back to the highway in this cold, and we have to be prepared for aftershocks. It's a miracle this little shack is still standing. I wouldn't want to assume we'll be so lucky next time."

Next time? Kennedy wondered why she'd ever come to Alaska. Why hadn't she listened to her dad? "What about the radio?" she asked. "Maybe we could try to signal for help."

Willow paused. "It's not a bad idea unless either Roger

or his fat, smelly partner are awake and feeling vengeful."

Kennedy thought back to the way the cabin had toppled in on itself when the tree fell on the roof. Had either Roger or Buster survived? Did they dare find out? "It may be worth trying."

"You're probably right. That radio might be our best shot. Even if we get to the highway, it's not like there's going to be a ton of traffic going in or out at this time of night. And if there were rock slides or anything along the Glenn, we could be totally cut off for weeks."

Kennedy wouldn't think about that right now. The biggest priority was to stay warm for the night.

And keep from starving.

"We can get some of the canned food, too," she suggested.

Willow nodded then looked back at Brandy in her corner. "I don't think she's fit to go anywhere. Not right now. When the aftershocks come, we'll have to get her out of the cabin though. At least in the open we'll have a chance to dodge the trees if they fall. But if the cabin goes down ..." She left the thought unfinished.

Kennedy took in a deep breath. "You stay here. I'll go back to see if I can dig out the radio and get some food. Anything else we might need?"

"Our coats, and blankets if you can find them. And batteries and flashlights. Who knows how long we'll be stuck here?"

Kennedy knew the answer to that at least. One night. Exactly one night. A night that was nearly over. All they had to do was survive the cold for a few more hours, and then when the sun came up, they'd make their way with Brandy back to the Glenn Highway and find the help they needed.

One night. That's all this nightmare was allowed to turn into. Just one night.

Willow took off her heeled boot. "You can't go out in nothing but a sock."

Kennedy had been so terrified during her run through the woods she hadn't even noticed the way her toes were burning with cold. She slipped on Willow's boot. There was something she still didn't understand. "How did you know about this cabin back here anyway?"

"I noticed it in the moonlight when I stepped outside with Buster. That's where Roger was coming from after he left the house. I'd already seen Brandy's pictures in that box and figured that if she were still alive, this is where he'd be keeping her. And I knew Buster was a phony with that message about my goat. He'd never called my family. All right. Do you still have my phone? You can use it as a flashlight." Willow frowned. "Or maybe we should go together."

Kennedy glanced at Brandy. "I don't think we better leave her alone. This is no big deal. I'll just get a few things and come right back." She forced confidence into her voice even though she felt none.

Willow reached out and wrapped her in a hug. "You be careful now, you hear? And if either of those men are still alive ..." Her voice trailed off.

As Kennedy stepped out again into the now silent moonlight, she tried not to ask herself what it was that Willow had been about to say.

CHAPTER 12

The night was now eerily quiet. No breeze. No rustling of leaves. No indication that just minutes earlier, the entire woods had threatened to collapse in on itself like Roger's rickety log cabin.

Kennedy knew where to go. She told herself that each time she second-guessed her footing and wondered if she was following the right trail. It felt like she and Willow had run a mile during the earthquake, but if Willow had spotted the cabin from Roger's place, it couldn't be nearly that far.

She wouldn't get lost.

Shining Willow's cellphone flashlight in one direction and then another, Kennedy thought back to all the wild animals that might live out here in the Alaskan wilderness. Polar bears weren't this low beneath the arctic circle, were they? No, if this part of the state was known for its polar bears, Willow would have mentioned it sooner.

What about other kinds of bear, though? Hopefully

anything out here would be deep in hibernation, but what creature could have slept through an earthquake like that? Kennedy was still dizzy, still trying to walk on shaky ground. It reminded her of the way she felt as a kid coming home after a full day at the waterslide park. She'd lie in bed, and her faulty proprioception would make her still feel like she was being tossed from side to side.

Faint moonlight shone on the debris from the cabin. Kennedy couldn't tell if she was trembling from cold or fear.

Get in, find the radio, get out. That's all she had to do. The radio, their coats, and a few cans of food. Hopefully something with a hint of nutrition. She could picture Willow starving before agreeing to taste spam.

After trying it earlier that night, Kennedy couldn't blame her.

She held her breath as she stepped onto the first creaky log of what used to be Roger's cabin. Half expecting his hand to reach out and grab her, she shined the flashlight all around, on the lookout for any sign of life. She wasn't sure which she was more terrified to discover — that the men who had attacked her and Willow were alive or that they weren't.

Beneath her, wood splintered loudly with each step she took. She scanned the debris. Where was the radio? She walked toward where she thought that shelf had been. What if the radio, their only connection to civilization, hadn't survive the quake?

No, she wouldn't panic. Not yet. It wasn't like they were in some remote island in a developing nation. This was the United States, with FEMA and all those other organizations meant to assist in situations like this. And wasn't the national guard involved too? Help would come. Kennedy would find their coats and the radio and anything else they'd need to make it through the night, and first thing tomorrow morning they'd be rescued.

They had to be.

CHAPTER 13

There. Thank God.

Buried beneath several cans of spam and layers of debris was the radio. Kennedy couldn't believe it was still intact. By the time she pried it out of the wreckage, the tops of both her hands were bleeding. She wasn't sure if that was from splinters in the wood or if her skin was just cracking away from the cold.

It didn't matter. They had their radio, their lifeline to rescue.

After finding their coats, she gave a little half-hearted hunt for spare batteries but soon gave up. Her hands hurt so much she realized she couldn't hold anything else in them anyway.

A bag. That's what she needed. Or some kind of blanket to use as a knapsack she could sling over her shoulder.

How cold was it out here? Negative what? And how long could she survive in this kind of temperature?

No, she couldn't be that pessimistic. She just had to keep moving. Keep moving and make it back to the little shed before her nose turned black and her fingers got frostbite. What if she needed her toes amputated?

Leave it to her overactive imagination to induce a major panic.

She wouldn't think this way. Her anxiety was behind her now. It was …

She dropped to her knees at the sound of the first roar. She heard it before she felt any movement beneath her. Not again …

It's just an aftershock, she told herself. *Just an aftershock …*

She glanced up, hoping that if any trees decided to land here she'd be quick enough to move out of the way. Her limbs were rigid, nearly stiff with cold. She didn't try to stand up or run when the earth began to shake. She would have to ride it out.

Just an aftershock …

There. It was over. That wasn't so bad. A person could get used to just about anything. Kennedy would get used to this too if she had to. But of course, this was only temporary. Just for the night. Maybe not even that long. Now that she had the radio, help was guaranteed.

Ok. She had her coat on. Before long, it'd start warming her up instead of stealing her body heat. She had the radio and some food. There was no way to carry everything, not with her hands balled up in her sleeves like they were. She shoved a few of the smaller cans into her pockets and figured she could come back for more if she really needed to.

Which she wouldn't because first thing in the morning — or sooner — they were getting rescued.

As much as she loved her roommate, she vowed to never visit Alaska again.

She was mustering the energy to start the cold journey back to Willow and Brandy when the second aftershock hit. This one was more intense. The ground didn't roll like it had in the initial quake, but it shook violently, like a dog thrashing its head from side to side while annihilating a chew toy.

The radio fell out of Kennedy's hands into a pile of rubble. She fell to her knees, praying it hadn't broken. The light caught on something. She screamed when she realized she was inches from Buster's fat, blotchy face. She scrambled back as the aftershock died down. Catching her breath, she kept her distance but shined the light toward him, looking for any signs of breath or life.

Nothing.

She wouldn't think about it. If she stopped to let reality sink in, she'd be too scared, too frozen to make it back to Willow and Brandy, who needed her. Brandy most of all. What had that poor thing lived through? And she was pregnant now. Kennedy didn't know much about childbirth, but she certainly could tell the difference between a baby bump and a swollen abdomen the size of a beach ball.

She had to get up. Had to forget about what she was leaving behind and return to Brandy with the food and the radio.

One step at a time. That's how she would get back. One faulty, unsteady step thanks to the uneven ground and Willow's ridiculous heel. She just had to ignore the fact that her feet were as cold as Buster's body beneath the rubble. Forget about the trauma she'd already endured. Survival meant pressing onward. There was no other way.

She just had to keep moving.

Couldn't stop ...

Why did it feel like the walk back to the cabin was taking so much longer? It's not like the radio was that heavy. The skin on the tops of her hands stung with cold and pain, but she wasn't so much of a wimp that a few cuts and scratches could slow her down.

Why was she so sluggish?

She wanted to rest, but knew she had to go on. It was too hard to hold Willow's cell phone while stumbling without exposing her hands to further cold, so she was relying on the light of the moon and nothing else. Maybe that's why it felt even creepier now.

Spookier.

Like the calm before a storm.

The only problem was Kennedy didn't know what disaster she was waiting for. Another aftershock? As long as they weren't any worse than the previous two, she'd be fine. They were terrifying reminders of the trauma of that first quake, but nothing that would put her in serious physical danger.

So why was she so nervous? Because she'd been attacked earlier? Because of what might have happened if she and Willow hadn't escaped those two drunk men? If that tree hadn't toppled down on Roger's cabin and freed them?

Wait a minute. That was it. Kennedy stopped.

Looked behind her.

Strained her ears in the nighttime silence.

She'd dug thoroughly around the wreckage hunting for that radio. She'd found Buster's body, but that was all.

So where was Roger?

CHAPTER 14

Her mind was playing tricks on her. That was it. Like kids who purposefully freak each other out telling ghost stories at summer camp until they can't go to sleep all night. It was all in her imagination. She was doing this to herself.

The reason she didn't find Roger was because he was buried so deeply in the debris. The reason he was buried so deeply was because he was a deplorable human being who had finally met God's judgment. Simple as that. She had no reason to be afraid. He was a nightmare, and that was all.

He didn't exist anymore.

Kennedy couldn't see the shed in the moonlight, but she knew she must be getting close. Just a few more minutes, and she'd be inside. Together again with Willow and Brandy, and before long, this entire vacation would be nothing but a terrible memory.

Just like Roger was.

Something sounded behind her. She refused to look. Refused to give in to her childish fears.

There it was again. A footstep?

No. It was nothing more harmful than a squirrel. Did they have squirrels in Alaska? Whatever it was, it couldn't hurt her. It wouldn't ...

"Get back here, girl."

Kennedy lunged ahead as if a few extra inches could save her from Roger's grasp.

His fingers grazed the back of her coat, but he couldn't hold on.

She surged forward, no longer aware of the cold but only of the burning in her lungs and the terror in her psyche.

A dream. A hallucination. She wished it were something that innocuous but knew from the pain as tree branches whipped across her face that she was stuck here in reality.

She had no other thought but to get to safety. Screaming now, as if the extra exertion could somehow lend her more energy.

Someone was standing in the doorway of the shed. Was Willow waiting for her?

She didn't know what else to do but run. That was her

only plan. Into the shed. If Willow was there, if she saw what was happening, maybe they'd find a way to barricade themselves in.

Closer now. She was shouting warnings, at least she thought they were warnings. Her brain was so focused on escape she wasn't even sure what she was saying. She just had to trust that Willow ...

Except it wasn't Willow in the doorway. It was Brandy. Her huge swell of a belly protruded out in front of her. She stood with one hand behind her back looking peaceful and serene.

"Out of the way!" Kennedy tried to yell. Had the poor girl lost her mind? Had her imprisonment driven her insane?

Kennedy raced past the threshold of the cabin, nearly plowing into Willow, who was waiting for her with outspread arms. She tried to pull Brandy inside, but Willow held her back. "Wait."

Roger stopped a few paces away from Brandy. "What are you doing off your wall, girl? Did I tell you to come outside?"

"I got scared. I was waiting for you. I thought something bad might have happened."

"Something bad will happen all right if you don't get back on that wall," he snarled.

Kennedy sank into the shadows but kept her mind focused and alert in case Brandy needed her help. Roger was drunk and couldn't have gotten out of that wreckage uninjured. The three of them could fight him off. They would find a way.

"Come on." Roger's voice was calmer now. Steadier. He took Brandy by the hand and led her as if she were a child to her chains. "You know this is for your own protection," he crooned.

"Yeah," she answered submissively. "I know. But before I go back on the wall, will you hold me for a minute? I got really scared. I thought you were hurt. Those two girls told me your cabin was destroyed."

He scoffed quietly. "They're just jealous. That's what. You don't pay them any mind, ok? You know I love you most. I always have, and I always will."

He wrapped his arms around her.

Kennedy glanced at Willow, wondering what they were doing waiting here in the shadows. If a pregnant girl wanted to allow herself to get chained back up on a wall in a shed that might collapse at the slightest hint of another aftershock, was there anything Kennedy or Willow could do?

"Hold me," Brandy pleaded. Her voice was so small, Kennedy thought she sounded more like a ten- or eleven-year-old than a grown woman. Pity gripped her soul and held her feet in place even while her brain begged her to run. She watched sadly while Roger held Brandy, murmuring kind words into her ear.

"You're so sweet," she said, but something in her voice had changed. Roger must have noticed it too. He pulled away as Brandy reached into his back pocket.

"This is for what you did to me." Brandy plunged his knife into his abdomen, pulled it back out, and hacked again.

CHAPTER 15

Kennedy didn't move. Just stood watching Roger's crumpled, bloody corpse and Brandy's expressionless face as she stared down at him.

Giving him a little nudge with her foot, Brandy asked, "Roger? You ok?" Her voice was sweet and childish again. "Roger?" She knelt down beside him. "I'm sorry. I didn't mean it."

Willow stepped forward and wrapped an arm around her.

Brandy jumped back. "Get away from me. You're the one who made me do this."

Willow didn't move. "It's all right, sweetie. You're safe now."

"I was safe with him," Brandy cried. "Look what you did." She stared at the body and recoiled as if she were seeing it for the first time. "Look what you did to him. You hurt him."

She pummeled Willow with her fists, but they landed

soft. Willow wrapped her in a hug. "Don't worry. Everything's going to be all right. We're all safe now. We're all ..."

Another low grumble from the pit of the earth. Kennedy couldn't keep her balance and fell to her knees.

"We've got to get out of here," Willow called out.

"I'm not leaving him!" Brandy clung to Roger's dead body. Kennedy and Willow had to exert all their strength to pry her away from the bloody corpse.

Outside the shed, Kennedy hoped this would be another small tremor, but the back and forth motion of the earth quickly morphed into the familiar undulating. Brandy shrieked when a tree branch whipped in front of her. Willow kept her arms wrapped around her protectively. Kennedy just tried to keep her balance.

"How long is this going to last?" Brandy shrieked.

Willow stood there stroking her hair while Kennedy worried all the movement was going to make her sick.

Willow was running before Kennedy could realize what the danger was. "Move it!" she shouted. "Hurry."

Kennedy blindly obeyed as her ears were deafened by a new sound, no longer the low rumbling but a deadly, angry cracking.

Brandy shrieked as the snow in front of them shifted.

"Hurry," Willow ordered, nearly dragging Brandy with her. The shed in front of them tossed from one side to the other as the snow around it collapsed in on itself.

"It's caving in," Willow shouted, still urging everyone further away from the crevice that was forming in front of their eyes.

"No! I can't leave him there!" Brandy turned around, and Willow and Kennedy both grabbed her arms before she toppled down the ravine that was swallowing trees and snow and everything else in its path.

"Roger!" Brandy shrieked as the cabin collapsed into darkness.

Kennedy and Willow dragged her away from the edge of what was now a cliff. It was too dark to tell how far down it went. Twenty feet? A hundred?

Brandy screamed and struggled free from Kennedy's arms. "I have to help him!"

"No, stay here," Kennedy shouted, but her voice was drowned out by the roaring earth. She lunged forward and grabbed Brandy's leg in time to stop her from jumping into the crevasse. Kennedy felt her own body starting to slip and knew she couldn't hold on for long. "Help!"

The earth gave one last defiant toss and then stopped. Kennedy's hands burned as she tried to keep her hold on

Brandy. "Help!" she repeated.

Brandy wasn't struggling. Was she all right?

Willow knelt beside her and grabbed Brandy by the hips. Straining together, they brought her back to the surface. Willow shined her light down the fissure, shaking her head. "Dude."

The crack that had opened in the earth and swallowed the cabin was at least as deep as the tallest trees.

"Dude," Willow repeated.

Brandy was crying quietly. Willow wrapped her arms around her. "We've got to find her someplace warm."

Kennedy didn't want to be the one to point out that they were miles from the road and hours from daylight. Neither of Roger's cabins had survived the earthquake and aftershocks. Where was there to go?

"What about the truck?" Willow suggested. "If we can get it running, we can turn up the heater and make it until morning."

Kennedy was thankful for some kind of plan. "Good idea. Then we can radio for ..." She stopped herself and looked down at the gaping scar in the earth where the cabin, along with the radio, now lay in heaps of rubble. "Never mind."

Willow rubbed her back. "Don't worry. We just need to

focus on warming up for a little longer. When the sun comes up, we'll make our way to the road. It's going to be just fine."

Kennedy nodded. They could do this.

Willow took Brandy by the arm. "Come on. Let's get you up out of the snow. Can you walk? We'll see if we can warm up in Roger's truck."

Brandy didn't respond. She had stopped weeping and was staring down at herself in wide-eyed bewilderment.

"What is it?" Willow's voice was full of compassion. "What's wrong?"

Brandy blinked once and continued to gaze at her lap.

"I think my water just broke."

CHAPTER 16

It was official. Kennedy was freaking out.

"We can't deliver a baby out here in the dark in the middle of nowhere!"

Willow tried to shush her. "Of course we can't. That's why we're going to take her to Roger's truck and get her warm."

"How do you expect to get her there? We can't carry her that far."

Willow raised her eyebrows. "You do know that women can walk while they're in labor, don't you? And that your water can break hours before you even start having contractions."

Kennedy didn't respond. When would she have ever learned that?

Willow wrapped her arm around Brandy. "Come on. The truck's not far. If we're lucky, we can drive you out of here. See how the roads are so we can get you some help. You're going to be just fine. Have you felt any contractions yet?"

"I'm not sure."

"It will be like cramps. Sometimes you only feel it in your back. And if you put your hand right here on your abdomen, it'll get hard. There, that's one now. Can you feel it?"

"A little."

"Good," Willow answered, although Kennedy couldn't dream up a single thing that was positive about their situation. Stuck in the middle of the woods, aftershocks destroying everything around them, and now they had a pregnant woman who was about to deliver a baby.

"We've got to get there fast," Willow was saying. "We don't want that amniotic fluid to freeze to your skin."

Kennedy didn't even want to know what that would look like and prayed they'd get to the truck on time. God had protected them this far. He'd just have to keep on watching out for them because Kennedy knew there was no way they could survive all the way until daybreak on their own.

By the time they got to Roger's vehicle, Brandy's pants were frozen stiff.

"I was afraid of that," Willow said and shined her flashlight around. A tree trunk had fallen across the back of the truck bed, and another one had flattened a four-wheeler that must have belonged to Buster. "Looks like we won't be driving out of here any time soon." She turned to Kennedy. "Can you look around for any blankets? I'll see if we can at least get the heater running."

"What about the keys?" Kennedy asked.

Willow chuckled. "This is the Alaska wilderness. Everybody leaves their keys in the ignition or on the dashboard. See?" She held up a single key on a chain and started up the truck.

Kennedy turned toward the cabin, feeling awkward on her uneven shoes. It wasn't until then she realized Willow was wearing nothing but her sock. "Your foot," she exclaimed. "I never gave you your boot back."

"Don't worry about it." Willow's face was drawn taut. "We were little busy back there."

"Yeah, but what about frostbite?"

Willow was coaxing Brandy out of her pants. "Worry about that later. Now go get some blankets. Please?" she added as an afterthought.

Kennedy remembered where Buster's body lay and made a wide circle to avoid him. She found the blankets without too much trouble and grabbed a few cans of spam, too.

"Any luck?" Willow asked when Kennedy returned.

"I got some blankets, but they're already frozen stiff. I don't know what good they'll do."

"Don't worry about that. Come in, and close the doors. I've got the heat running. Here. You sit on top of the blankets and get them warmed up for us."

It didn't seem like much, but Kennedy was thankful for something she could do to feel useful.

"Ok, the contractions aren't all that regular. It could be a while before anything starts to happen, and there's a good chance by then we'll have found some way to get help. Is this your first delivery?"

Brandy nodded. "Roger said he would take me to the hospital. He said everything would be ok."

"He's right. You're going to be fine," Willow assured her. "Kennedy, why don't you pray for us. Is that all right with you?" she asked Brandy.

Kennedy's rear end was freezing from sitting on top of the blankets, which could explain why she sounded so stubborn. "First, we need to look at your foot. You shouldn't have been running around in just your sock."

Willow shrugged. "Yeah, well, you don't always think things through when you're trying to stay alive."

Kennedy tried to think of something that might lighten the mood but couldn't. "Let's just take a look."

"I don't know what it is you're expecting to see." Willow stretched her leg across Brandy's lap and hoisted her foot onto Kennedy's knee. "Here it is. See? It's a foot."

Kennedy felt it. The sock was frozen stiff. "Should you take that off?"

"Go ahead. You're the one all worried."

Kennedy aimed the flashlight. "I don't know what I'm looking for," she confessed. Willow's toes were red, but other than that they looked just like toes. She wasn't sure what she was expecting. Tiny black stumps where the cold had already eaten away the flesh?

"See? I'm fine." Willow swung her leg back down and felt Brandy's midsection. "There comes another contraction. You tell me when they get real uncomfortable."

Kennedy still wasn't ready to ignore Willow. "Shouldn't you wrap it or something so it gets warm now?"

"Probably."

Kennedy took Willow's boot off her own foot.

"Here. Put this back on. I don't need it anymore."

Willow sighed. "Fine. But I'm only doing it so you stop worrying about me."

As if Kennedy would ever stop worrying at a time like this.

She hugged her arms around her, wondering how long it would take for the truck to heat up, wondering how long the night would last, wondering what they would do if Brandy's baby decided it was ready to be born before help arrived.

CHAPTER 17

"What time is it?" Kennedy rubbed her eyes. She hadn't meant to doze off, but she soon came to realize that childbirth was nothing like the movies where your water breaks and in minutes you're screaming and writhing in agony. With nothing better to do, she had leaned up against the window and let exhaustion overtake her.

Willow swept some hair off Brandy's sweaty brow. "Almost eight. You were out forever. I'm glad you got that sleep. You really needed it."

Kennedy felt guilty for not being more useful. "How are things going? Is she doing ok?"

Willow smiled faintly. "You can ask yourself, you know. It's just labor. It's not like she can't talk."

Kennedy felt herself blush. "Ok, how are you feeling?"

Brandy winced. "Contractions are starting to hurt now."

"She's in the transition stage," Willow explained. "The good news is her body's figuring out what it needs to do just fine. I wouldn't be surprised if she'll start pushing soon."

"What? Don't we need to take her to the hospital?"

"First of all, the hospital wouldn't do anything for her but throw on a bunch of monitors and push an epidural that she doesn't need. But if we were in town and had access to a midwifery, then yes, we'd take her there, but did you see that tree? The entire back half of the truck is pinned down, and even if we found a way to lift it off, we wouldn't be able to get very far with the tail end dragging on the ground. Anyway, women have been delivering babies without men in white coats telling them how to do it for millennia. So what I need you to do is promise me that you won't freak out, and if I ask for your help, you just have to tell yourself to get over any nerves or squeamishness or anything else, buckle down, and do what I say. Got that?"

Kennedy swallowed down a wave of nausea and nodded.

Willow held her gaze. "I'm dead serious. You don't freak out on me, and you do exactly what I need you to do when I need you to do it. Have you ever seen a live birth before?"

Kennedy was sure that whatever blood she'd had left in her brain had rushed to her feet by now.

Willow shook her head. "Never mind. Just remember, when you're a doctor, you'll have to do all kinds of more stressful things than this. So here's your crash course. Ready? And you listen too, Brandy, because I think your time's coming up. When it feels like you need to push, that's your body telling you what to do. Kennedy and I are going to do our best to keep you squatting over the seat. You put your forearms here like this, and one leg on my knee and one leg on Kennedy's knee, and that way you'll have gravity on your side. When the urge comes, it'll feel like you're making a really big poop. I'm not going to try to put it in any nicer language than that. You're going to feel like you're forcing out a ten-pound piece of poop. You've probably seen in the movies where the mother screams and yells and thrashes around wasting all her energy, but that's not what you're going to do. You're going to stay nice and quiet and focus all your strength on bearing down. Not yet. Your body's not quite ready, but it will be soon, and when that happens, you just let us know, and Kennedy and I'll be here ready to help you. You can do this, right?"

Brandy's voice was choppy. "Do I have a choice?"

"No, you don't. But don't worry about that. Your body knows just what it needs to do. Kennedy, you ready? I want you to sit right there, and, Brandy, you put your knee on top of hers so it will sort of be like you're squatting. In between contractions, you just sit back down on the seat and try to get some rest. Are you doing ok? Are you warm enough?"

"I think I have to pee."

"That's totally normal," Willow said. "Here, Kennedy, hand me that coffee cup."

Kennedy was trying to convince herself that now would be no time to faint. Willow was right about one thing. As a doctor, she'd have to help people in all kinds of situations just like this, except she'd always planned to do it in a warm, sterile hospital room, with clean clothes, gloves, and plenty of nurses to assist.

"I think it's starting." Brandy's voice was tense.

"Just lean up here." Willow helped her rest her forearms on the dashboard. "Lean up here and when the contractions come, we're going to lift you up off the seat a little bit, and you follow your body's cues. This is going to be just fine. Kennedy, why don't you pray for us?"

It wasn't until then that Kennedy detected the hint of fear in Willow's voice. She would never get over how good of an actor her roommate could be.

Praying out loud would at least focus her attention on something besides the sweating, laboring woman squatting on her leg. "Dear God, thank you that you're always with us. Thank you that you've kept us safe so far."

Kennedy wondered what else to say. Her breath was

choppy, and she hoped that it wasn't an indication that she was about to have a panic attack. She remembered what Willow said. She'd be in lots of situations even more stressful than this as a doctor, and she'd have to stay rational. Have to keep her brain from shutting down.

"Lord, please help Brandy's baby to be just fine. Help everything to go really smoothly. Help her to not be in too much pain."

Kennedy had to pause every few sentences and think about what she wanted to pray for next, but she always found something. After praying about everything she could think of for Brandy and the baby, she prayed for Willow and then for Nick and then for all of Willow's family in Copper Lake, and before she knew it she was praying for anybody who might have been injured in last night's earthquake.

She didn't stop there, either. She prayed for the whole state of Alaska. Right about the time she began praying for her parents and their ministry to North Korean refugees living in China, Willow interrupted with a loud, "This is it. Kennedy, get ready."

Kennedy didn't know exactly what she was supposed to be getting ready for, but she immediately stopped talking and held her breath.

"Come on, Brandy," Willow coaxed. "One or two more

pushes and it will all be over."

Over? What was Willow saying? Was Brandy's baby really about to ...

Brandy let out a loud grunt, Willow reached her hands down between her legs, and just as Kennedy felt sure she was going to pass out, a sound like a cat meowing snapped her out of her near panic.

"Here she is," Willow crooned. "She's absolutely perfect." Her tone switched from gushing to demanding. "Kennedy, the blanket."

She handed Willow the blanket, thankful her brain was still in control of her body.

The baby cried faintly while Willow sang out, "Are you cold, little sweetie? Here. I'm just going to wrap you up like this, and then we'll let your mama keep you nice and warm. What a good baby. You did such a good job being born."

Kennedy wasn't sure if Willow had said something funny or if she was just disoriented from the stress, but she sensed now would not be an appropriate time to laugh and clenched her jaw shut.

"You did so well," Willow told Brandy. "Your baby is so proud of you. Look how she's watching you. Do you know what you're going to name her?"

"I was thinking something like Rylee."

"That's a pretty name." Willow leaned down and sang out in a high-pitched voice, "Hi, little Rylee. Hi, sweet baby." She looked again at Brandy. "You can go ahead and talk to her. She knows your voice."

"I don't know what to say."

"Tell her what a good baby she is. Tell her what a good job she did. Tell her anything that's on your mind."

Brandy leaned over her newborn, nuzzled her cheek, and whispered, "Your daddy will be so excited to meet you."

CHAPTER 18

Brandy was exhausted and fell asleep with Rylee on her chest almost immediately after delivering the placenta.

"What happens now?" Kennedy asked.

"When they wake up, it will be important to get Brandy nursing, but other than that, I think we're just fine."

"I was talking more about everything. The truck, the earthquake. How much longer before daylight?"

Willow chuckled. "Daylight's already here, Miss Observant. Sun came up about half an hour ago."

Kennedy looked out the truck window. "Oh."

"But in answer to your first question, I don't think Brandy can walk all the way to the highway after what she's gone through. That probably means one of us should stay here and one of us should head toward the Glenn to see if there's any way to get help."

"I can do that."

"I think you'll have to." Willow smiled. "Unless you've

117

become an expert at breast-feeding and are ready to give Brandy and her baby a crash course."

"No, you stay here. But how do you know so much about all this anyway, delivering babies and nursing and everything else?"

Willow shrugged. "I've always been there when the goats and sheep are born. Usually, everything goes just fine, but sometimes you have to step in and help. Plus my mom's coached a few women around Glennallen who wanted to have home births. The clinic there won't deliver babies, so if you get pregnant, you either have to spend the last two or three weeks of pregnancy in town so you'll be close to medical care, or you plan on a home birth. Mom took me to a few of them when I was a teenager. Ninety percent of it is just keeping the moms from freaking out." She grinned. "And keeping your assistant from freaking out, too."

"Yeah, I'm sorry I wasn't better help."

"Don't say that. You did great. Who would have thought that a crazy, Type-A germaphobe like you could have handled a delivery in a truck without completely losing your head? You should be really proud of yourself."

Kennedy wasn't sure if she was being complimented or insulted and changed the subject. "How's your foot?"

Willow shrugged. "I'm fine. Here, you take the boot

back. And take my coat on top of yours. You'll need it more than I do. I'll have to turn the truck off for now. We're running kind of low on gas. You know how to get back to the highway from here? You just follow the tire tracks in the snow."

Kennedy nodded. If her roommate could safely deliver a child in the middle of nowhere, Kennedy could walk a few miles without getting lost.

"So you sure you don't mind heading out alone?" Willow asked. "It will be kind of long you know. You should eat before you go."

"I'll grab something from the cabin, or at least what's left of it."

Willow shook her head. "All that will be frozen. Didn't you bring a few things back into the truck last night?"

"Yeah, I think there's a can of spam around here somewhere."

Willow grinned. "Bon appétit. And even if it's totally gross, you'll need the calories to stay warm. You probably don't have to worry about it, but you know the basics about hypothermia, right? You'll go from just shivering and cold to really exhausted. At that point, it messes with your brain. It will make you want to just sit down and sleep, and you'll tell yourself it will only be for a few minutes, but you've got to make yourself keep going, right?"

Kennedy couldn't believe she was actually getting a crash course in hypothermia in the middle of the Alaskan wilderness.

Willow gave her a reassuring smile. "Don't worry. You'll be fine. You can follow the tire tracks so you won't get lost, and you won't have to worry about going through the deep snow. Hey, you ok? You look like you're about to cry."

Kennedy shook her head. "This wasn't how I expected to be spending the day before your wedding."

Willow sighed. "Yeah, you and me both."

CHAPTER 19

Kennedy took a deep breath. She could do it. Her job was easy. Just follow the tire tracks to the Glenn Highway and signal for help. She didn't think about what she'd do if the roads were deserted. Maybe even impassable. God hadn't spared them from Roger's murderous rage and ensured Brandy's safe delivery in order to desert them now.

Help would be there.

It had to be.

The tire tracks made an easy path through the snow. Kennedy was glad she didn't have to wrestle her way through the two- or three-foot drifts. A few times, she came across a tree that had crashed along the path, but otherwise the woods appeared completely normal.

If you could call anything about watching the sun coming up at 10:45 in the morning normal.

She tried to remember how long they'd driven last night. After hitting the moose, she thought making it all the way to Roger's cabin would be the hard part. So much had happened since then. Was it really less than twelve hours ago?

She started to pray, thanking God for keeping them safe, but her thoughts were distracted. Wondering what would have happened to her and Willow if the earthquake hadn't saved them from their assailants. Remembering the way Brandy had rushed at Roger and then thrown herself on his corpse. Kennedy had never seen anyone sound so grief-stricken. So remorseful.

But if Brandy hadn't attacked Roger ...

It was silly to dwell on what hadn't happened. It wouldn't help her get to the Glenn more quickly.

She and Willow were supposed to be waking up in a nice heated Anchorage hotel and starting their five-hour drive to Copper Lake. Not battling insane attackers or delivering babies in negative temperatures.

She kept her fists balled up in her sleeves and cursed Willow's stupid boot. Did her roommate own any foot apparel with less than a three-inch heel?

Well, it was better than nothing. Besides, if it hadn't been for Willow stepping up last night and taking control, Kennedy didn't want to imagine what could have happened to her, Brandy, or the baby.

She wondered how badly the earthquake had hit the surrounding regions. With Anchorage reeling from the volcano, would the earthquake confirm people's fears that the world really was about to end? What about those riots her dad was so afraid of?

What would happen to Willow's wedding plans? Even if Kennedy found help, was the highway passable? What if they couldn't get back to the Winters' home? What about the wedding? With the earthquake as bad as it had been, was Copper Lake even standing anymore?

She wished she could check the news on her phone. She hadn't realized until now how accustomed she'd grown to having access to the internet all hours of the day. But even if she had her cell right now, there wouldn't be any reception. No way to signal for help or find out how badly the rest of the state was hit.

The only thing to do was go forward. Keep pressing on. She knew if she stopped to think, she could come up with one or two highly effective Bible verses. Metaphors comparing this trek of hers through the cold and the snow to the Christian walk of faith. But she didn't have time to stop and think.

She had to keep moving.

Her whole body was trembling. Even with Willow's

extra coat, she wasn't prepared for a five-mile hike through the woods in temperatures like this.

How could Willow have grown up in this state and survived?

She thought about Brandy, wondered what she must have suffered from the time of her kidnapping until now. Would she ever recover from that trauma? There had been something so primal, so animalistic about the way she threw herself on Roger's body. It was easier to think of her as some nameless character, an animal in a cage, than a human being. A human being who'd once had dreams and joys and hopes for her life.

What had Roger done to her?

And what would it take to bring the real Brandy back up to the surface?

God, she's been through so much ... It wasn't fair. How could Kennedy try to wrap her mind around it? God could have kept Brandy from getting kidnapped. How hard could that have been? There would have been hundreds of opportunities. Let Brandy develop a cough. Make the coffee stand close down early that night because they ran out of espresso beans. Give a few other strong, hardy, and well-armed Alaskans the urge to get coffee or late-night snacks at the same time Roger was planning to abduct her.

Better yet, he could have thrown a moose in the path of Roger's car to keep him from getting to Brandy in the first place. Or stopped him a dozen other ways. Kept him off whatever trajectory turned him into the kind of psychopath who would go around kidnapping girls and handcuffing them to the walls of abandoned cabins out in the middle of the woods.

He could have made it so that Roger was never born.

An infinite number of possibilities — all of them preventing Brandy's abduction. Where would she be now? Preparing to marry the love of her life? About to graduate college? Working her way up the corporate ladder to land herself the career she'd always dreamed of?

It wasn't right. No matter how Kennedy looked at it, nothing was right. God could have stopped Roger. He was strong enough.

So why didn't he?

And what about Brandy's baby? Innocent little Rylee. What had she ever done to deserve being born in such squalid, terrifying conditions? If God loved all people equally — and who could read the Bible and come away believing anything else? — why did he allow some people to suffer such unthinkable trials and others to live relatively pain-free lives?

She was too cold to come to any real conclusions but figured the questions would still baffle her if she were relaxing in a steaming hot sauna. Some things would probably never make sense, but she wouldn't stop trying to figure them out nonetheless. Somewhere there had to be answers, and even if she never came up with a satisfactory explanation for life's injustices, at the very least she could work to try to alleviate them.

It was an overwhelming task to consider. How many other girls like Brandy were living victim to the whims of villains and sociopaths? How many were caught in the clutches of prostitution and sex slavery? It was so easy to think of things like that happening in other parts of the world, but here was an unforgettable reminder of the kind of suffering that happened regularly in her own country.

Was there any place safe left on the earth?

She thought about a conversation she'd listened to one morning around the dining room table with her pastor and his family. Sandy was reading from one of their devotional books and came across a quote. *The safest place you can be is in the center of God's will.*

Pastor Carl scoffed. "Yeah. Tell that to the Christians who are imprisoned in North Korea for their faith. Or the evangelists getting beheaded in the Middle East."

Sandy was quick to show her disappointment. "I think what it's saying, love, is that when we're doing what God has called us to do, we can trust him to watch out for us and protect us."

"Except for when he doesn't," Carl added dryly.

Sandy rolled her eyes and leaned over toward Kennedy. "You have to forgive him, sweetie. He's been getting mood swings ever since he had that accident."

"It's not a mood swing," Carl insisted. "It's the simple truth. *Everyone who wants to live a godly life in Christ Jesus will be persecuted.* Second Timothy 3:12. You don't get much more clear-cut than that."

Sandy frowned. "Well, of course there's persecution and suffering, but when a Christian is doing the will of the Lord ..."

"The Lord just might see fit to let them get fed to lions," Carl interrupted.

At that point, their son Woong, who previously had been absorbed in his food, jumped into the conversation. "Wow, fed to lions? Does that really happen, Dad? Do the lions eat them all up and then throw up their bones like an owl? Or do the bones go into the digestive tract and turn into poop? Do you think you could go to the zoo and look at lion poop and see if maybe they've fed a Christian to him or not?"

Carl and Sandy never finished their theological debate.

Kennedy still didn't know what to think of it. There were so many verses in the Bible that talked about God keeping his children safe, but nearly all of the original apostles and so many early Christians died in gruesome ways. Sawed in half, crucified upside down, burned at the stake ...

Kennedy shook her head. These certainly weren't the kinds of thoughts that made her trek through the woods any easier.

Find your happy place. That's what her counselor was always telling her to do to overcome her anxiety. Think about the things that made her feel truly safe and joyful. The problem was all her good memories from the past few years were tainted by the fear and trauma that went along with them.

Did Kennedy have a single happy memory that was untarnished by sadness or danger?

She thought about Willow's wedding. It was nearly all her roommate had talked about last semester. But what if something had happened to Nick? What if Willow's home had collapsed in the quake? No, she had to hold onto hope. It's what gave her strength to keep on putting one foot in front of the other. She reminded herself how deeply in love Willow and Nick were. How obvious it was that they were destined to marry.

And hoping that one day God would bring a soulmate into her life as well.

Preferably someone who wouldn't abandon her because he was HIV-positive or wouldn't die saving her from a crazy terrorist with a bomb.

Or a journalist who flew across to the other end of the world and didn't even think to send a text.

There she went again. She had probably kept happy images of Willow's wedding in her brain for all of twenty seconds before her mind wandered to her own unlucky love life. No wonder she was anxious all the time with that many negative thoughts.

So instead of trying to focus on joyful memories or hopeful dreams, she directed one foot in front of the other. That was the only way she'd keep from collapsing with cold and exhaustion.

She had to keep going.

Willow and Brandy and little baby Rylee were counting on her.

Time was passing, but the scenery looked exactly the same. She had to be getting closer to the highway now. There were no landmarks to back up her optimism, but she couldn't make it much farther. Not with her toes stinging like she'd stepped on fire and her gait still unsteady because of her roommate's stupid heeled boot. Even with her hands tucked up into the seams of her coat, the tops cracked open, and the blood froze immediately to her skin. Something rattled in her sinuses every time she inhaled so she wasn't sure if she was breathing through frozen boogers or if her snot had literally turned to ice.

Rest. Just a few minutes. Two or three at most. How long had she been out here anyway? The sun was so low on the horizon it was impossible to guess the time. It had been just after dawn when she started walking, but the sun was still so low it could be getting ready to set by now and she would have no way to tell the difference.

Keep walking. That's what she had to do. She couldn't stop.

She tried to think about what she'd do when she found warmth. There was a happy place. A hot shower — that was something she could imagine. That hope alone gave her strength to keep going.

And then came the shaking. Funny. She thought she had already been shivering, but it was nothing like this. She tried to wrap her coat more tightly against her, but her fingers had grown numb. She couldn't grasp anything.

The road turned right just a little bit ahead. She'd make

it to that curve, and then she'd let herself rest.

But her legs wouldn't cooperate. How can you walk in uneven boots when your toes have lost their feeling? How can you keep pressing on when your body's shivering so hard you're panting from all the extra exertion? How can you force yourself into action when your brain's higher functions are shutting down with each passing step, each dropping degree?

And the road stretching so far ahead ...

Keep going, she told herself. *Don't stop moving.*

But her body wouldn't listen. She was still focusing on her happy place.

Hot showers. Steaming mugs of hot chocolate.

The snow was so soft. Soft and downy. A mattress and a pillow and a blanket all at the same time. Piles of blankets stacked three feet high.

That's what she needed.

She just had to stop and catch her breath.

Just a minute or two ...

CHAPTER 20

Roaring fireplaces.

Sandy's homemade cookies being pulled out of a piping-hot oven.

Electric blankets turned on high and piled on top of her.

Sunbathing on a Florida beach on vacation with her parents.

Hot. So hot.

Why was she wearing this coat? She had to get it off ...

"Kennedy!" She didn't want to wake up. Not yet. What was Willow doing here, ruining her perfect dream?

Come to think of it, what was Willow doing here at all?

"Kennedy," Willow snapped. She sounded mad. Kennedy should apologize. She hadn't meant to lie down in the snow.

Where were those cookies? The blankets?

"Wake up right now, and hold this baby while I try to get

a fire going."

"There already is a fire," Kennedy mumbled. If she could just remember where she put it ...

"Come on, Sleeping Beauty. Snap yourself out of it and do it now. I'm not joking. I swear I'll slap you if you don't wake up and look at me. "

"I'm awake."

"Look at me," Willow demanded.

"Ok. Sheesh." Kennedy tried to say something about being bossy, but her words were garbled.

"I told you to open your eyes and look at me."

"I am looking at you."

"No you aren't. How many fingers am I holding up?"

"I don't know."

"Kennedy. Open your eyes. Wake up. You need to take the baby so I can make a fire."

"... Too hot for a fire."

Something bit her cheek. "Ow." Kennedy blinked.

Willow was staring, her hand still upraised. "You awake now?"

Kennedy nodded and rubbed her sore face. "I think so."

"You gonna be able to hold this baby?"

Every thought Kennedy tried to process had to make its way through a wall of Jell-O. "Why am I holding the baby?"

She stared at the newborn Willow had placed in her arms. Rylee was wrapped in blankets so that only her nose and eyes were visible.

"Because if I don't make you a fire, you're going to want to go back to sleep, and no matter what happens, no matter how cold you feel, you've got to promise to stay awake. Promise?"

"I wasn't cold. I had blankets."

Willow ignored her and started making a pile of twigs and branches. "I found a box of matches back at the cabin. Just give me a minute or two and we'll get you warmed up, all right?"

Rylee yawned in her sleep. Kennedy started to giggle.

"What's so funny?" Willow sounded cross. Was she mad Kennedy hadn't made it to the highway?

"The baby made a face."

"Yeah, well just hold her tight. You guys need to warm each other up while I get this fire going."

Willow struck two or three different matches before the pile lit. "Here." She took Rylee, bundled up in all her blankets, and nudged Kennedy closer to the small flame.

"I don't feel it." Kennedy frowned.

"Yeah, you're probably already numb. It was stupid of me to send you out here by yourself."

"I never made it to the road. I'm sorry."

Willow shook her head. "Don't be. We'll get you warmed up, and then we'll go together."

Even though Kennedy's body couldn't feel the warmth from the fire, her brain began to slowly clear up, like a car's windshield with the defroster on. "Where's Brandy? Did you leave her back at the truck?"

Willow let out her breath. "A lot's happened while you were out here trying to nap in the snow. Brandy's dead."

CHAPTER 21

Every ounce of mental fog cleared away in an instant. Kennedy leaned in a little closer toward the flame. "Are you serious? What happened?"

Willow shifted Rylee over her shoulder. "She got freaked out by the last aftershock. I think something in her brain just snapped."

Kennedy frowned. "What aftershock?"

Willow stared at her. "You didn't feel it? How long were you asleep?"

"I don't know."

Willow shook her head. "You're really lucky I got here when I did. You know that, don't you?"

Kennedy wasn't thinking about her own health or safety. "So what happened with the aftershock?"

"Brandy jumped out of the truck. Set the baby down on the seat and made a run for the shed. You should have seen her go. I tried to stop her. I really thought I was going to get there soon enough, but she got to the edge of that cliff and just dove in. She was screaming for Roger the whole time." Willow shook her head. "I went after her. I know it was a stupid thing to do, leaving the baby alone in the truck like that, but I thought that maybe if I hurried I could get her to safety or something. But she was gone. Didn't survive the fall."

"How'd you get back out?" Kennedy asked.

I followed the fissure a little ways to where it wasn't so steep. Used the roots of a tree trunk to pull myself out."

Kennedy didn't know what to say.

"I would have gotten here sooner," Willow remarked, "but for as many times as I've seen my mom teach other women how to tie a sling, I couldn't for the life of me figure out how to make one for Rylee. Plus these shoes are huge."

Kennedy looked down and noticed Willow's boots for the first time. "Where'd you get those?"

Willow didn't meet her gaze. "They were Buster's. I know it's gross, but I needed something. Couldn't walk all the way down here in a sock."

Kennedy was ashamed that she hadn't even thought to ask about Willow. "I totally forgot about your foot. Are you ok? Should you take your shoe off so we can look at it?"

Willow shook her head. "I know what it's going to look

like. You don't need to worry about me."

"But you might have ..."

"I'm fine. Hearty Alaskan chick, remember?" Willow smiled. "And I hate to say it, but we shouldn't stay here too long. We've used up over half of our daylight already, and I don't want to sound like I'm being melodramatic, but I don't think any of us are up to spending another night out here in the cold."

"I still say we should take a look at your foot to make sure that ..."

Willow shook her head. "We're getting really close to the Glenn. I still have some matches, so we can build ourselves another fire if we need to once we get there. Are you ready? No more naps?"

Kennedy tried to smile back. "No more naps."

Willow took in a deep breath and squared her shoulders. "All right. Let's get moving."

CHAPTER 22

Kennedy was grateful to have Willow by her side. Without her roommate's constant encouragement, she would have been tempted to lie down for another rest.

"How you doing?" Willow asked.

"Aside from freaking out about nearly dying in the cold, I'm great."

Willow smiled. "You don't need to worry. There's no way God's finished with you yet."

It was the same thing Pastor Carl said so many times about how certain he was that he wouldn't die until God had allowed him to complete the work he'd started here on earth. But how could anybody be so sure? How could you tell if God was finished with you or not? And where in the Bible did he promise not to allow people to die until they completed the tasks he had assigned them?

Kennedy didn't know. She was still trying to figure out how you could know what God's plan for your life actually was. Carl talked about certain mentors in his life suggesting that he had the gift of preaching. Willow and Nick spoke as if they'd known from nearly the first day they met that God wanted them to get married. They still hadn't solidified their post-wedding plans, but they were treating the next few months as a big adventure where God would lead them one step at a time.

Is that what he expected Kennedy to do, too? Was it possible that she'd wake up tomorrow morning and the Holy Spirit would tell her *I want you to be a missionary in Cambodia*, and all of a sudden she would be expected to drop out of school and forget everything she'd worked so hard to achieve?

Is that how God worked?

What about people who never received a clear calling from God in the first place? Was it just that they weren't listening? Was there one exact path every believer was supposed to take, and if they veered to the right or to the left just an inch, it would ruin their God-given destiny? If that were the case, how could any believer go forward with any life plans? Wouldn't you be constantly crippled with doubt? Paralyzed with fear that you might go the wrong direction?

Kennedy wished she knew. She hated not having a plan, which is why Harvard's early acceptance medical program had been such a good fit for her. She signed the papers the summer after her junior year of high school, and the next decade of her life was organized and arranged.

Then Harvard had rescinded their offer, only to reinstate it after threats of legal action. Months later, Kennedy still wasn't sure what she should do. After watching Willow deliver Rylee, recalling those waves of panic, she was beginning to wonder if she should go into medicine at all. What if the stress was too much to handle?

So much for her perfect laid-out future.

But maybe now wasn't the time to set out her ten-year plan. She was tired and cold and exhausted. Not to mention hungry. She was in no state to be thinking about anything clearly.

"I really hope Nick's ok," Willow said, breaking the silence. "I wish there was a way to jump online and find out how bad that earthquake was."

Kennedy didn't respond. If she wanted to keep up her strength and optimism, thinking about last night wasn't the way to do it.

"Kind of makes you wonder, doesn't it?" Willow asked.

"Wonder what?"

"You know. About all those end of the worlders and their pickets and pamphlets and things. Didn't they say earthquakes would be part of it?"

Kennedy shrugged. "I could run around naked on TV screaming that there's going to be a tornado in the Midwest, and at some point in the next year my prediction's going to come true, right?"

"Yeah, but why don't you prophesy with your clothes on like a normal nut-case?"

Kennedy let out a chuckle. "I'm just saying the whole thing's silly. Jesus says that when he comes back, nobody's going to be able to predict when it will happen."

"But he does say something about earthquakes, doesn't he?"

"Yeah, but there have been earthquakes at least since the time of Noah, right?"

"I don't know. Aren't you the Bible expert?"

"Hardly. But I do know that we're not supposed to get all freaked out when people tell us when or how the world's going to end. Only God knows that, and when it happens, there's nothing we can do to try to stop it."

"There's something that doesn't make sense though." Willow readjusted Rylee in her arms.

"What's that?"

"Well, Jesus says there's going to be wars and stuff, right? That it's going to get worse before it gets better."

Kennedy tried to remember if there was an actual verse about that. "Basically. That's what I've heard."

"So here's my question. Why do we bother at all? Why do we go on the mission field and risk our comfort and safety when things are destined to go to hell anyway, if you pardon the expression? Why do we work at ending slavery or pray for peace in the Middle East or march against poverty? If things have to get that bad before Jesus can come back, if they're going to get that bad no matter what, why don't we throw up our hands and stay in our safe little bubbles and hide our faces in the sand like good little fatalists? Nick's been talking about starting up a home for victims of sexual abuse and human trafficking, and after everything with Brandy, I could totally see myself jumping into that kind of ministry. But if the Bible tells us that the world's going to continue getting more and more wicked and violent anyway, why should we bother?"

Kennedy was embarrassed to admit that she'd never asked herself that question before. She had definitely grown more aware about the suffering and injustices around her than she'd been as a naïve little freshman, but had that information changed her? She always said she'd like to be involved in some kind of mission work when she became a doctor, even if it was only volunteering for short-term trips, but was that just a copout?

With so many people suffering right now, should she really wait another five and a half years or longer before she tried to help any of them?

She had the feeling that if her feet weren't so numb, if her hands weren't cracked open and bleeding from exposure, if her nose wasn't so cold that it felt like she was breathing through shaved ice, she might be able to offer Willow a more thoughtful response than, "That's a really good question."

Rylee let out a grunt in her sleep.

"Is she ok?" Kennedy had never been around a newborn before and had no idea what noises they were or weren't expected to make.

"The blankets are keeping her warm enough for now. I wish she'd wake up, though. I don't think it's a good sign that she hasn't acted the least bit hungry yet."

"How far do you think we are from the road?"

Willow sighed. "Let's just hope and pray we're close."

CHAPTER 23

Kennedy would have never guessed she could walk so fast given how exhausted and cold she was. Her lungs stung from panting, but all that exertion paid off. After rounding a corner, the Glenn Highway came into view.

"Thank you, God," Willow breathed.

Kennedy's sentiments exactly.

"We've got to find some place to warm Rylee up." Willow surged ahead.

Kennedy strained to keep up.

"Listen!" Willow called behind her. "There's a car coming. If we hurry, we'll make it."

Kennedy couldn't run. It wasn't possible. *Please God*, she prayed, *please tell the car to stop.*

"Hey!" Willow shouted at the passing vehicle. "Hey! Slow down. Wait!"

She reached the edge of the road as the sound died away. The car was gone before they'd even spotted it.

"Gobstoppers," Willow exclaimed.

Usually, Kennedy laughed at her roommate's creative choice in exclamations, but there was nothing humorous in this situation.

"Just a few seconds too late." Willow shook her head. "I've got to sit down."

Kennedy didn't argue. The girls plopped onto a snow drift on the side of the highway.

"Guess we should make another fire," Willow finally declared. "I swear I don't even have the energy. That car ..."

Kennedy let out her breath. She was still thinking about the speeding vehicle, too, their one chance of rescue.

"We can't stay here very long," Willow said. "It's too cold, and there's no telling when anyone else will make their way down here. We could go back down toward where we totaled the car, try to run the heater some, or we go the opposite direction and try to make our way to Eureka."

"How far away is that lodge they were talking about?" Kennedy asked. The idea of an actual heated room to sit down in, or a bed with blankets to pile on top of her, was almost too luxurious to fathom.

"From here? About fifteen miles. There's no way we'd get there by sundown, but maybe we'll run into someone on the way. Then again there's nothing to stop for between here and Eureka. Any cars coming or going that direction will come by here first anyway."

"So we wait?" Kennedy asked.

Willow frowned and felt Rylee's cheek. "We can't just sit here. I say we make a fire, get as warm as we can, then we go to where we crashed the car and pray the heater's working. I hate to say it, but that's probably our only option right now."

"Maybe someone else will come down this way," Kennedy added.

"You can always hope." Willow stood up. "All right. Can you hold her while I get another fire started? Just keep her as close to you as you can. And turn this way so your back's to the breeze. I'm not sure …" She didn't finish her sentence. When Kennedy looked at Rylee's listless face, she was able to guess what Willow was thinking.

"A fire would be really good," Kennedy agreed.

Willow's voice fell flat. "It's our only hope.

CHAPTER 24

"Too bad we don't have any marshmallows," Willow chuckled once the fire was blazing.

Kennedy wondered how her roommate could keep up a cheerful attitude in spite of how cold and exhausted they felt.

"What else do you have to eat?" Willow asked.

Kennedy felt in her pockets. "I think there's still a can or two of spam."

"I swore I'd never touch this stuff." Willow grimaced. "If it weren't the last resort ..."

"Don't worry. It's probably all synthetic, right? Not even real meat at all?"

Willow laughed. "That's what I'll tell myself. So should we pray?"

"Should we what?"

"Pray. You know. Thank God for the food. If you could even call it that." She bowed her head and began without waiting for an invitation. "Dear God, thank you for keeping us safe to this point. Thank you that you know exactly where we're at and what we need. Please bless this food, even though it's full of nitrates and sodium and a whole lot of other ingredients that I don't even want to guess at right now. Please use it to strengthen us for the hours ahead. And watch over Rylee. Help her to ..."

Willow's voice caught. She adjusted the baby in her arms and tried again. "Help her to be ok, Lord. Please. In Jesus' name, amen."

Kennedy added a quick prayer of her own, and the girls each opened a can of spam.

Willow wrinkled her entire face as she took a sniff. "I really need the calories, don't I?"

Kennedy nodded. "Just pretend you're doing it for an acting class."

"Ha. There's a thought." Willow peeled a tiny bit of meat off and examined it between her fingers. The bite was no larger than a pea. "I guess I don't have any other choice. Well, didn't Jesus at one point say that all food was clean if you're thankful for it or something? Isn't that somewhere in the Bible?"

Kennedy shrugged. She hated to admit it, but her roommate was already more familiar with Scripture than she was.

"Well, thanks, God, for the spam." Willow brought the crumb slowly to her mouth but stopped. "Dude. Listen."

Kennedy strained her ears. She heard it too.

"Is that …"

Both girls jumped to their feet.

"Another car!"

Kennedy stepped into the road and waved her hands frantically. There was no way they were going to let their chance at rescue pass them by again. "Wait!" she called out. "Help!"

Willow ran out behind her, holding Rylee in her arms. The car slowed to a stop. Willow was laughing so hard Kennedy worried she had gone hysterical.

"Look who it is!" Willow exclaimed and nearly tripped on some ice, rushing to the driver's side.

The door opened. Nick stepped out and threw his arms around his fiancé.

CHAPTER 25

"How did you find us?"

"Where have you been?"

"Whose baby is that?"

"Are my parents ok?"

"Are you hurt?"

Once they put out the fire and crawled into the heated car, Nick gave a quick run-down of how he'd discovered them. "The earthquake woke us up last night. Woke everybody up. I tried calling your cell but couldn't get through. I started hearing stories about riots in Anchorage. I guess those folks in the doomsday camp were really going crazy. I was afraid you'd get caught up in the middle of that, so I borrowed your parents' car and started driving.

"About five miles down the road, I saw the wreck. Talk about freaking out. So I stopped, thinking maybe you were in the woods somewhere and in trouble. I hunted around for a little bit, couldn't find you, but then I remembered passing a lodge a little bit earlier, so I thought I'd go up there. See if maybe you'd found your way to shelter. You have no idea how worried I've been."

Willow was sitting next to Nick, her legs curled up against her chest and her entire body burrowed into his. "Our story's a little longer than that." As they headed toward Eureka, she gave Nick the abbreviated rundown of their night, downplaying how much danger they'd been in before the earthquake hit.

Nick listened with wide eyes. He was so attentive even his dreadlocks held still. "I can't believe you delivered a baby all by yourself."

"I didn't." Willow turned around to smile at Kennedy, who was holding Rylee close in the backseat. "Kennedy was there to help."

It wasn't until they reached the Eureka Lodge that Kennedy's brain began to realize just how lucky she was to be alive. Moriah, a plump middle-aged woman who owned the establishment, brought in bowls of warm water for their hands and feet, set up three different space heaters, and covered everyone in blankets fresh out of the dryer.

Thankfully, within half an hour of their arrival, Rylee woke up and her fierce screams let everyone know she was ready for something to eat. After a couple phone calls, Moriah tracked down a local family who had baby formula as well as diapers.

"I can't believe I'm willingly bottle-feeding synthetic milk to a baby," Willow remarked.

Kennedy figured her roommate didn't want to be reminded about how close she'd come to eating spam either.

After her bottle and a change of clothes, Rylee was wrapped up again in even heavier blankets and went directly to sleep.

"You doing all right?" Willow asked Kennedy.

She nodded. Moriah had put salve on the cracked skin of her hands. Kennedy's fingers and toes burned as they thawed, but she was thankful for the chance to warm up.

It was Willow who had everybody the most concerned. "My feet are just mad at me for making them so cold," she remarked with a confident chuckle, but half an hour later after soaking in increasingly hot water, two of her toes remained black.

Moriah called the Glennallen clinic to ask what they should do.

"She's just being over-protective." Willow waved her hand dismissively. "It's what happens in Alaska when things like earthquakes hit. Everyone comes together, helps everyone else out whether they need it or not." Another chuckle, this one not so bold or self-assured.

While they warmed up with bowls of Moriah's hearty soup, Nick filled them in on what had happened in Copper Lake.

"Your mom ran out to check on the animals when the earthquake hit. I guess she was a little worried about the whole barn collapsing, but it was ok. You should have heard the chickens though. Even above the noise from the quake, I could hear your rooster crowing his head off."

Willow smiled. "That's Bach for you. He's such a drama queen. How did the goats do?"

It was good to hear Willow chatting about the farm animals she loved. Good to be wrapped up in blankets, surrounded by friends and strangers who were concerned for her well-being. Maybe too concerned, but Kennedy wouldn't worry about that right now.

When they were ready, Nick would drive them to the Glennallen clinic so the nurse could check out Willow's foot. There was a trooper station there too where they'd tell the officers what they knew about Brandy's kidnapping and figure out what they should do about her baby.

After Moriah filled their tank with gas and packed thermoses of soup for the road, they wrapped themselves up in extra winter gear donated by the generous folks of Eureka, piled into Nick's car once more, and made their way up the Glenn.

CHAPTER 26

"Yes, Mom. I'm sure I'm fine."

"Well, I've just been scared sick about you as soon as I heard about that earthquake. I told you that your dad and I had a bad feeling about this trip. All those weirdos claiming it's the end of the world. You've seen the news? They're rioting all over Anchorage."

Kennedy didn't bother to tell her mom that she'd been too busy running from attackers, dodging falling trees, and trying not to die of hypothermia to worry about what was going on in other parts of the state.

"I'm just glad you finally got hold of us. I called Willow's home yesterday. They said they hadn't heard from you either. Your dad and I have been so worried. You really need to call us or at least send your dad a text when things like this happen so we know if you're ok."

Kennedy guessed that if her mom had any idea how much of Alaska went without any cell coverage at all, she'd never consent to Kennedy visiting here again. "I'm sorry you were scared."

"But everybody's well now? You didn't catch a cold or anything?"

"Nothing like that." Kennedy was warm for perhaps the first time since she landed in Alaska, and her appetite had returned with a vengeance even after two bowls of Moriah's chicken noodle soup.

"And Willow? Is she with you right now? I hate the thought of you being out there all alone."

"She's in the exam room next door. She got some pretty bad frostbite on her toes. They may have to take her to Valdez."

"Why? What's in Valdez?"

Kennedy sighed. "The hospital."

"Oh, dear. And what about the wedding? What's going to happen?"

"I have no idea. Right now with her toes ..." Kennedy didn't finish her thought.

"Well," her mom said, "I'm glad you're all right. You should call Carl and Sandy too and let them know you're safe. You know they worry about you almost as much as your father and I do."

"I will. What's Dad doing, by the way?" Kennedy

couldn't remember the last time she'd gotten herself out of an emergency situation and didn't have him there on the other line asking questions and giving directions about what to do next.

"Didn't I tell you? We have company." There was something teasing in her mom's tone.

"Oh, yeah?"

"Yes. A nice young man. He'd stand out in a crowd of a thousand because of his bright red hair, but I suppose you already know that about him."

Kennedy ignored the way her gut flapped and flopped like a landed fish. "Ian's there? At our house? What's he doing?"

"He's interviewing your father for a documentary he's making about North Korean refugees."

"Dad can't go on record with stuff like that."

"Don't worry, your friend's got a super high-tech camera, you know. He can blur the face, distort the voice. It will be perfectly safe."

Kennedy hoped so. She didn't like the thought of worrying over her parents' safety. Talk about role reversals.

"Anyway, your dad's just come out now and says that somebody wants to talk to you."

Kennedy took a deep breath to try to steady her nerves.

She told herself that the only reason she was feeling anxious was because of all the danger and suspense she'd experienced since last night. "Hello?"

"Kennedy. It's me, Ian. Nice house you've got here."

She still couldn't picture Ian in her parents' home. "Thanks. Haven't heard from you in a while." Why was that the first thing she said? Would he think she was accusing him?

"Yeah. This trip's been quite a bit busier than I planned, but I've had a great time enjoying your mom's baking and sitting and visiting with your dad."

"Hi there, Kensie girl," her dad called out. Was she on speaker phone? "What's shaking over there in Alaska? Besides the tectonic plates, I mean."

Hearing her dad's voice made Kennedy realize how much she wished she were at home right now.

"Anyway," Ian said, "I was talking to your dad about a program I'm going to be part of this year. There's a group in South Korea involved in rescuing and resettling North Korean nationals, and they're holding their first-ever summer camp for some of the resettled refugees in June. I'm going to go work on my documentary there, but like I mentioned to your dad, it would be really nice if I had someone who spoke Korean to serve as an interpreter."

"You're asking me to recommend somebody?"

"No. I'm asking you to come spend next summer with me in South Korea. What do you think?"

"It'd be a great opportunity, Kensie girl," added her dad.

Kennedy was glad there was no one around to see her blush. "Let me think about it, ok?"

"Sure. Take your time. And I know you've had your share of excitement, so I promised your dad that if you do agree to go, I'll make sure you have a perfectly safe, uneventful trip. Deal?"

She chuckled. "Sounds good to me."

"All right, princess," her dad cut in, "you've had a long day and need some rest now, but call us if anything else happens and keep us posted about everything over there. Tell Willow we're all praying for her. You know about aftershocks, right? And stay out of coastal areas. I don't know if they're expecting any tidal waves, but you don't go near the water."

"I'll be careful, Dad." For this time at least, Kennedy didn't mind all his unsolicited advice.

"I'm glad you called," he said. "You stay careful, all right? And tell Willow's parents hi. They sound like real nice folks each time we talk."

"They are. I'll be sure to pass the message on to them."

"Talk to you later."

"Ok. Bye."

Kennedy unwrapped her blankets and slipped on the pair of fur-lined boots one of Moriah's friends from Eureka had donated. She walked cautiously to the examining room next door and was surprised at how many people were inside.

Willow's parents, two nurses, a trooper, and a social worker in a professional business suit who was holding baby Rylee. Willow sat with her feet in a hot bath while Nick tightened the blankets around her shoulders.

"Thank you so much for answering all our questions," the trooper was saying. The conversation stopped when Kennedy entered.

"I'm sorry," she stammered. "I'll come back later."

"No, come on in." Mrs. Winters held out her arm and gave Kennedy a hug. "I'm so glad you're safe," she whispered, giving her cheek an air kiss.

The trooper put his notebook in his back pocket. "We'll probably have more questions for you before long. Just make sure to keep your cell with you so we can be in touch."

Willow nodded. "What's going to happen to Rylee now?"

"The baby?" the trooper asked and turned to the woman in the suit.

"We'll do our best to find some relatives. I don't believe there were any immediate members in the mother's family, but we'll do some research. Try to find someone."

"What about until then?" Willow asked.

"She'll be put in a temporary foster home that's equipped to handle infants this young. She'll be perfectly ..."

"What about us?" Mr. Winters interrupted.

"I beg your pardon?"

"My wife and I have taken in emergency foster placements in the past. You still have our records on file. Go ahead and look us up. Judson and Star Winters."

The social worker looked at Willow's mom. "And you'd be interested in the placement, then?"

Mrs. Winters nodded. "Absolutely. Unless my daughter's worried about how it will affect her wedding plans."

Willow smiled. "You know, I was always a little disappointed I never found a flower girl. You think Rylee's up for the job?"

CHAPTER 27

"Those bread rolls turned out delicious," Star told her husband.

It was Kennedy's second Christmas Eve dinner at the Winters' home in their Copper Lake homestead. She couldn't believe how fast time had flown since the earthquake.

Judson, who was holding baby Rylee on his lap, put his face close to hers and cooed, "It's too bad our sweet little baby girl can't eat the big yummy bread yet, but she can't because it would hurt her tummy wummy, wouldn't it?"

His wife let out a sigh. "I still think it's ridiculous that we have to give her bottled formula when we've got two perfectly healthy milk goats. Makes me remember why we don't foster full time."

He smiled and continued to talk in his baby voice. "No, but soon she'll grow big and strong and when she's a year, she'll be able to drink all the goat's milk she wants, won't she? Won't she?"

Star laid a hand on her husband's arm. "Just remember, there's a decent chance she won't be with us in a year. They haven't found any family members to take her in yet, but how hard do you really think they're looking with the earthquake causing as much damage as it did and it being the week before Christmas?"

He ignored her remark. "She'll stay with us because she wants to grow up on good, healthy goat's milk. Not the nasty stuff that comes in plastic containers from the store."

Nick cleared his throat. "This is a delicious dinner. Thank you so much."

Star turned to him and offered a smile just as dazzling as her daughter's. "Of course. You're our son now."

"Or will be," Judson added while glancing at his watch, "in about half an hour."

"What time's the pastor coming over?" Star asked.

"Right about six."

Willow smiled from her seat beside Nick. "I'm just glad everything worked out so well in the end. We had to wait a couple extra days, but I don't mind. I think the idea of a church ceremony was stressing me out anyway."

Kennedy doubted Willow had ever felt true stress for an hour out of her entire life, but she didn't say anything.

Nick stood up. "Well, if you'll excuse me, I'm going to

carry my wife-to-be upstairs to her room so she can get ready."

"I can get upstairs by myself," Willow insisted. "They just cut off two toes, not my whole leg."

Nick grinned. "I'm especially glad about that tonight of all nights."

"Cut that out." Willow pushed him playfully away. "Kennedy, hand me my crutches, and then *you* can help me get ready. Nick's got to stay down here and pretend like he hasn't seen me all day."

"Oh, wait." Judson held up his hand. "Before you go, we have a new Christmas Eve tradition at our home, don't we? Isn't somebody supposed to read the Christmas story and then we'll sing a hymn? That's how we did it last year."

"You really want to do that, Daddy?" Willow asked.

"Of course. You're a Christian now, and so is my future son-in-law. What kind of dad would I be if we ignored something important like that?"

"I left my Bible in the guest room. I'll go grab it," Nick said.

Star leaned over and hugged Willow. "I'm so excited for you," she whispered. "He's such a good man."

"I know, Mom."

"You're going to be so happy together."

"You've got that right."

164

CHAPTER 28

After Nick read Luke 2 and everyone sang *Silent Night*, Star began clearing the table while her husband asked Nick about the exact date of Jesus' birth.

"Come on," Willow whispered. "That's our cue to go upstairs and get ready."

"Sure you don't want me to carry you up?" Nick asked with a grin.

"After the wedding," Willow answered, her voice full of teasing.

Kennedy handed her the crutches, and they both went upstairs.

"How are you feeling?" Kennedy couldn't remember seeing her roommate look so peaceful and happy before.

Willow sank onto her bed. "I don't even know how to describe it. It's like I've been expecting Nick my entire life. Like I've known him forever and have just been waiting for God to bring us together. It's like living out a fairy tale."

Kennedy smiled and took down the dress Willow had picked from her closet. "You sure you don't want to go big and fancy?"

Willow smiled. "I'm sure. In fact, now that the big day's here, I almost regret letting my hair go natural again. I think I had this certain picture in my head that a bride had to look an exact way, but that's really just me being vain. Nick didn't fall in love with me because I could fit into an expensive white dress or revert back to plain old brown hair. I mean, if he'd shaved off his dreadlocks for this wedding, I might have called the whole thing off. Not really, but you know what I mean."

Kennedy smiled and helped Willow into her cotton tie-dyed dress that looked more appropriate for a summer fair than a Christmas Eve wedding.

The doorbell rang. "That must be Pastor Reggie," Willow said. "I'm so glad he agreed to come do this, especially with it being Christmas Eve and all. I guess the good news about having to postpone the wedding for a few days is that it's going to be wicked quick."

"How do you know that?" Kennedy asked.

"Because he's got two young kids, and he wants to get back home as soon as he can, I'm sure. And with as long as

Nick and I have been waiting to do it right, I'm not interested in a two-hour ceremony before I'm able to take him to bed and make him mine forever."

Kennedy had been listening to Willow and Nick's innuendos for nearly a week. She wasn't even embarrassed anymore. She held out the pair of crutches. "You ready?"

Willow smiled. "Dude. Let's do this."

CHAPTER 29

The wedding was as unique and beautiful as Willow and Nick's love for each other.

Willow was a ray of colorful sunshine in her rainbow dress. Nick wore a T-shirt with a picture of Solomon proclaiming his love to one of his brides. Kennedy couldn't remember the exact quote from Song of Solomon, but it had something to do with comparing his beloved to a cow.

If the Copper Lake pastor was surprised by the unconventionality of the ceremony, he didn't show it. Kennedy figured that informality must somehow play into Alaskan culture, since even Pastor Reggie showed up in jeans and flannel. Baby Rylee was the most dressed up out of everybody in a white baby gown that had once belonged to Willow's grandmother. Unfortunately, she slept through the procession, and Willow never did get the flower girl she'd been hoping for.

Pastor Reggie kept the ceremony short and simple. Willow and Nick had written their own vows, and after they exchanged the rings, Pastor Reggie led them in a heartfelt prayer. After he asked God to bless their union, they signed the marriage license, and Pastor Reggie went home, taking several dishes full of leftovers to share with his family.

"Well, now," Willow's dad announced, "it's taken me twenty-one years to say this, but I finally have a son to call my own. Welcome to our family." He gave Nick an embrace large enough that it nearly swallowed him up.

Willow and her mom were both wiping tears off each other's faces, and Kennedy felt more than a little out of place.

Judson cleared his throat. "And now, a toast to the happy couple. Willow, I know that you're a grown woman, fully confident in your capabilities, fully assured of yourself, but there's a part of me that's always going to look on you as my Willow Willow Armadillo, the little girl who tried bungee-jumping off the chicken coop when she was seven and had to wear a leg cast for two months one summer. And now you're in a cast again, but you're not letting that slow you down. And I'm sure at some point you'll look at your feet and wish that you could get all ten toes manicured so you can show them off in those cute little sandals you like to buy, but instead of feeling sad or ashamed, I hope you'll always realize how proud we are to have a daughter who would sacrifice herself not only for her friend but for a perfect stranger who needed you. Little Rylee may not have survived if it weren't for you, and we have no idea how long she's going to be part of our family, but she's already made it so much richer. It's been over two decades since we had someone this little to share Christmas love with.

"As for you, Nick, I mean it when I say I couldn't wish for a better, more suitable spouse for my daughter. You and Willow complement each other so well, and I'm not ashamed to admit that you've taught this old dog a few new tricks. I had no idea there were Christians who were so committed to social justice and freedom. You put every single liberal who makes sweeping generalizations about how all Christ-followers are bigoted racists to shame, and I'm glad you proved them and me wrong.

"As for you, Willow Willow Armadillo, I'm speaking for your mother and me both when I tell you that we are so happy you've found a relationship with the divine that has obviously made you so happy and fulfilled and given your life a new purpose. And whatever crazy adventures the universe throws your way, I want you both to know you always have a home for you here in Copper Lake.

"Which is why we want to talk to you about your wedding present. You're down-to-earth, folksy kids. My guess is as long as you have food and shelter and Willow has a little pocket money to spend on her hair dyes and manicures, you won't have a care in the world. But your mother and I have talked it over, and we've decided it's time. We're splitting up the homestead. Willow, you're getting your grandpa's old cabin and half of the hay field, including the income it generates. Nick, I don't know how good you are with tools, but if you don't mind a little sweat and blisters, I guarantee you that over the summer we can make it not only livable but a place you can truly call home. But it's yours to do with whatever you like. Your mom and I mean that. You can sell it and go abroad for a few years, you can rent it out and finish up college, you can stay here and raise goats or chickens or grandbabies or whatever. It's entirely up to you. Our only stipulation is that you are both in perfect agreement with each other with whatever decision you make."

Willow wrapped her arms around her dad's neck and gave him and her mom noisy kisses on their cheeks, while Nick looked almost as shocked and woozy as if he'd just seen a needle coming straight at him.

"You guys are the best," Willow said and picked up her glass. "To the most wonderful family in the world."

"You sure you're supposed to be the one giving the toast?" Mr. Winters asked.

"Just drink with me," Willow laughed. Everybody obeyed.

CHAPTER 30

Kennedy looked outside the window of Willow's room while she waited for the call to go through. Star was outside, bringing eggs in from the coop.

"Merry Christmas. You've reached the Sterns."

She stared at her phone to make sure she dialed the right number. "Ian? Is that you?"

"Yeah. Don't sound so surprised. Knowing your mom, do you think she'd let a friend of yours spend Christmas all alone in a big, foreign country?"

"You're at my parents' again?" She still couldn't get the picture to settle in her mind.

"Yeah. Your dad's calling out merry Christmas in the background if you can't hear him, but he and your mom are stuffing sausages or something like that so they can't talk. Want me to put you on speaker phone?"

"No," she answered quickly. "I'll call back in a little bit. Or just tell them to call when they're free."

"How are things there?" Ian's voice was easy, like he had nothing better to do than hang out in Kennedy's parents' kitchen and talk to her from the other side of the world.

"Good. We just finished Christmas breakfast. Willow and Nick had to postpone their honeymoon plans until they fix the highway, so we're all here."

"You doing all right out there? Your dad and I were looking at a map last night. You're really cut off."

So he was there last night too? Had he moved in?

"It's ok. The Winters have a big pantry, and they grow or raise most of their own food, so it's not that bad for us, but it's causing a few problems for other folks around here, especially the ones who have to get into town for medical appointments."

"How are things in Anchorage?" he asked. "I haven't heard too much lately. Are the riots over?"

"Yeah, I don't think anyone had the heart to keep up the looting over Christmas, but the city's a pretty big mess. I think the last count was around fifty confirmed dead from the quake. Most of that was in Anchorage."

"Wow. I'm glad you're ok."

"Me, too."

"Well, your dad's cleaning up now, so I'm sure he'll want to talk to you, but before he does, have you thought any more about that summer camp in Seoul? I think it could be a really neat opportunity for us both."

Us both? She wasn't quite sure what he was saying but tried not to read too much into it.

Did she want to spend her summer in South Korea working at a camp for resettled refugees? It wouldn't build her premed resume. She still hadn't decided if she was going to stick with Harvard or apply to other med schools over the summer.

Or was medical school a dream of her own making? A dream that God was going to ask her to give up in exchange for something even better?

Did she dare take time off to volunteer at a camp for people she didn't even know and would never see again? Did she want to spend the summer away from her own family?

Kennedy took a deep breath. "You know what? I think I'll do it. I could use a change of scenery."

She could hear Ian's smile on the other end of the line. "Perfect. It's a date. I'll let you talk to your dad now."

"All right. Merry Christmas, Ian."

"Merry Christmas, Kennedy."

A NOTE FROM THE AUTHOR

I hope you enjoyed Kennedy's most recent adventure! It was certainly fun for me plunking her down in my own home state of Alaska.

One of the things that makes these Kennedy books so exciting for me to write is the feedback I get from you. Your comments, reviews, and encouraging emails bring so much momentum to this project, and I'm really thankful for that!

Of course, Kennedy has more adventures ahead of her, and I hope you follow her through them all. You might also want to check out novels from my other series. The *Whispers of Refuge* books deal with underground believers in North Korea and will give you the opportunity to meet the Sterns (Kennedy's missionary parents) more thoroughly. My *Orchard Grove Women's Fiction* novels are set in Washington but also share characters with the Kennedy series, as do my *Sweet Dreams Christian Romance* books.

You'd think I'd have learned this lesson pretty well by now, but each novel I write serves to remind me how helpless I'd be without the Holy Spirit. I'm also so thankful for the prayers that help bring these books to life.

My husband is a huge encouragement to me, and I'm also very grateful to my editors and beta readers for saving me from a lot of embarrassing mistakes. Thanks also to Victoria for the great cover. You're a joy to work with.

If you ever want to be in touch, you're welcome to contact me, sign up to request a free novel, or check out all my titles at alanaterry.com.

DISCUSSION QUESTIONS

For group discussion or personal reflection

Ice Breaker Questions

1. What's the coldest temperature you've ever been in?

2. Have you ever been in a major car accident?

3. What's the most dangerous natural disaster you've lived through?

4. Which do you think is scariest: flood, earthquake, tornado, or other natural disaster?

5. Do you read much end-of-the-world fiction (either Christian or secular)? Why do you think these books have such an appeal?

6. Have you read the book of Revelation?

7. What's your own personal attitude toward the end times? *Hope I'm not there, it'll all work out in the end, it's gonna be really terrible, Christians won't have to live through it anyway*, etc.

Story-Related Questions

1. Kennedy is faced with a lot of questions about her future in this novel. What path do you think she should choose?

2. Do you think God has one specific life plan in mind for each believer or do you think we are free to make our own decisions as long as they don't go against Scripture?

3. What do you expect Willow to do with her future? How do you feel about the decisions she's made up until now?

4. Have you ever met a new believer who's grown as quickly as Willow?

5. What is your opinion about Willow's parents? Are they a couple you'd like to meet?

6. How do you react in emergencies? Are you calm and collected or do you tend to freak out?

7. If you were in the same situation as Willow and Kennedy, would you have reacted any differently?

Books by Alana Terry

Kennedy Stern Christian Suspense Series

Unplanned, Paralyzed, Policed, Straightened, Turbulence,
Infected, Abridged, Secluded, Captivated

Orchard Grove Christian Women's Fiction

Beauty from Ashes

Before the Dawn

Breath of Heaven

Sweet Dreams Christian Romance

What Dreams May Come

What Dreams May Lie

Whispers of Refuge (Christian suspense set in North Korea)

The Beloved Daughter

Slave Again

Torn Asunder

Flower Swallow

See a full list at www.alanaterry.com

Printed in the USA
CPSIA information can be obtained
at www.ICGtesting.com
LVHW040902070624
782373LV00003B/100

9 781941 735619